Dunzy's Coffee Shop

R. E. Henderson

Copyright © 2018 R. E. Henderson

Edited and Cover art by Rachel Henderson

This is a work of fiction. Names, characters, places, and incidents either are the product of the authors' imagination or are used fictitiously, and any resemblance to actual persons, living or dead, business establishments, events, or locales is entirely coincidental. The publisher does not have any control over and does not assume any responsibility for authors or third-party websites or their content.

ISBN:
ISBN

DEDICATION

This book is dedicated to nerds and lovers of coffee.

Contents

ACKNOWLEDGMENTS

I want to give a special thanks to my wife, Rachel, for supporting, editing, and painting the cover art of this book. She's a huge inspiration to me. And I would like to thank Bobby and Sheri Hartzog from Sassy Pants Sweets & Treats, as well as Andy and Ashley Mrozkowski from Pedal Java for supporting this book and allowing me to make cameo appearances of them. I love you all.

Prologue

(2020)

A cool breeze followed behind Todd Clinton as he entered Dunzy's Coffee Shop. He shook off snow from his jacket as he suddenly felt the warm and comfort of the shop. As he took off his toboggan and scarf he noticed the dying embers in the fireplace.

The gentleman behind the counter in a green apron, washing mugs, said, "Welcome to Dunzy's Coffee Shop, how many I-" The man stopped mid-sentence and then continued. "Well, how about that? I don't believe it. How have you been, Todd? Sit down, sit down."

Todd gave him a look of utter confusion and had no clue who the man was until he stepped closer. "I'm sorry

Charlie, I didn't recognize you there for a second. Your gray hair threw me off for a bit."

He tossed his jacket on a stool at the counter before taking a seat and pulling out a pack of cigarettes. Charlie took notice and said, "Sorry, but there's no smoking in here."

"Right."

Charlie said, "Would you like some coffee? I'm about to close, so it's a little cold. But that's the joy of a microwave."

"Yeah, sure." Todd stared down at the counter.

"So, how've you been?" Charlie asked as he poured a cup and put it in the microwave.

"I've been alright, how about yourself?"

"Pretty decent, I can't complain."

"Cool, cool." Todd looked around, "So, this place yours? Or are you just working the low salary this beloved town has to offer?"

"Hey, this town isn't that bad-better than what it used to be. I must be doing pretty good for myself since I own the place."

The microwave dinged, and Charlie handed Todd the mug.

"Thanks."

There was a moment of silence between them as Todd drank his coffee, then he said, "Man, this stuff is really good. You've got something good going for you."

"Thanks man."

Todd took a big swig and said, "Well, I guess I better head on out."

"Why the rush? You just got here, stay awhile."

"Na man, that's okay. I'll see you around. How much for the coffee?"

"For you, no charge."

"Good deal, have a good night."

Just like that, Todd was out the door just as fast as he came in. Charlie picked up the still warm mug and noticed he had left his scarf on the stool.

Chapter One

(2020)

As gravel crunched underneath his tires, Todd, pulled up to his childhood home. There was an uneasy pain in his stomach, he sure didn't want to be back here. Years have taken its toll, the house- faded and chipped paint on the exterior, part of the gutter hung low, and though the grass was brown and dead from the winter, it was knee length high and poked out through the snow.

He made his way up the steps as slow as could be, both not to slip and fall on his rear end on frozen ice, and also not to fall through the rotten wood. Each step he made was an echo in the night, on top of the screech from the screen door that entered the porch. He didn't want to wake his dad, but a voice in the dark startled him to where he stumbled anyways not to fall off the porch, "Well, look who it is."

"Dad? Wha- what are you doing out here? It's freezing. Come on, lets get you back inside before you freeze to death."

"I'm fine, death doesn't bother me, it's only inevitable. How about instead, you come take a seat beside me. We won't be out here too much longer, your aunt Lana will be coming to get me shortly."

"I don't blame her, have you seen how much snow is out here? Surprised you don't have pneumonia yet."

"No, that was last night."

"Wow." Todd lit a cigarette and pulled his jacket tight.

"You're the one to talk of death, son. Those right there will kill you one puff at a time."

"Yeah, well, so will driving through the Halls community, but we still have to do that every day."

"Good point." They sat in silence for a moment, his dad taking in the night. "Beautiful night tonight isn't it?"

Todd stared down at the floorboards, his mind elsewhere. "Do what?"

"Beautiful night, isn't it? Boy, you must be older than I am now, not hearing me very well."

"Sorry, I was deep in thought."

The smile his dad had from seeing his son quickly faded. "What kind of trouble are you in Todd?"

"What makes you think I'm in trouble?"

"You haven't been home in years and then, you show up with a receding hairline and smoking. I get the vibe something's bothering you. Come on, son, I'm smarter than you think. I'm old, but not senile...well, much."

"There's no trouble, I just-"

The front door swung open and an older woman in a bathrobe stepped outside. "I thought I heard someone out here. Todd, is that you?" Aunt Lana asked.

"Yes ma'am, it's me."

"You men come on inside and get warm."

"Will do," Todd said. He helped his father up from the swing where headlights shined on them as it came up the drive.

"More guests? My, people are out late tonight." Aunt Lana said as she took over with Jim.

Todd stood alone as he watched Charlie get out from his car and make his way up to the porch with his headlights still on. "How's it going Charlie? Can't get enough of me?"

"You left your scarf at the shop."

"Oh…thanks." Todd took the scarf and then offered Charlie a cigarette.

"No thanks, I don't smoke."

Todd shrugged and put the pack back in his pocket. "Suit yourself."

"Look, Todd, what's going on with you man? You seem really…different. Distant, maybe."

"Charlie, I just don't want anybody to know I'm back in town. Or, at least, know *why* I'm back. It's pretty personal."

"You know you can tell me. We've gone way back."

"We do go way back, but man, I just…forget it." Todd went inside and slammed the door behind him, leaving Charlie alone on the porch steps. He was gone by the time Todd made his way up to his bedroom.

Even his bedroom hasn't changed in the years he had been gone. Movie posters still hung on the wall which gave him a resemblance to his once teenage years. Icicle lights hung from ceiling. And yet, despite him being gone, the room was kept clean and tidy along with an aroma of Pine-Sol. Aunt Lana had kept it dust free for him.

He had laid his bag on his bed, just as he had done every day when he came home from school. He stood for a moment while he took in the many adolescent memories- whether they were good or bad. One picture frame in particular caught his eye, the one of Charlie, himself, and a girl named Hannah. The memories of his past stayed with him wherever he went, but Hannah he unfortunately forgotten about. When young and full of life, she had meant the world to him, but now she was just a spec in his memory.

It didn't take long for him to fall asleep. As much as he didn't want to be home, he was more relaxed than he had been in a long while. But it was the thunder that woke him in the middle of the early morning at 3:25 A.M. He pulled back the curtain to see only the light from the street lamp next to the barn and an icy rain that bounced off the window. He laid back down and was out once again.

Chapter Two

(2020)

It was the smell of fried bacon, eggs, and hash browns that awoken Todd. The storm from the night before had passed and left a fresh coat of snow and ice on the ground. Still dressed in his pajamas, and no real big plans for the day, Todd went down stairs.

Aunt Lana turned off the stove as she heard Todd step in. "Well good morning, Hunny. Have you some breakfast." She sat down at the table herself, apron still around her waist.

"Dad not up yet? That's hard to believe. Usually he was up before the sunrise."

"Yeah, he's been sleeping a whole lot more here lately- constantly tired and weak. He's not doing well, Todd."

"I didn't figure he was."

Todd pulled out his pack of cigarettes from his pajama top pocket, about had one lit when Aunt Lana cut in, "Not in this house you won't. Your mother would kill you if she knew you were smoking in her house...let alone, smoking at all. So would your father if he were able."

"Yeah...sorry." He glanced down at his plate of food in front of him and burst into laughter of the smiley face made out of bacon, eyes made of eggs, and hair out of hash browns. "What in the world is this? Am I 6?"

"Nope, just thought you needed a good laugh."

"I did actually, thank you." He contemplated on praying a blessing over his food, but instead, just dove right in.

"Alright, Todd, you know me- I'm pushy. Lets beat around the bush for a moment, why are you back?"

"What? I can't come home to see my family without being interrogated?"

"Yes, but, it was you who I think wanted to get out of this town. And now here you are sitting across from me out of nowhere and you expect me not to believe that there's something going on? *Something*."

"There's nothing going on, I promise. I mean, there is, but it's nothing serious. Nothing to stop the press over."

"So you're not in any trouble are you? Drugs? Money? Anything like that? You're not dying are you?"

"Nope, none of that. Is it personal? Yeah."

"Your girlfriend isn't pregnant is she? Don't tell me, you, of all people are running away from the responsibilities of being that baby's father."

"Well, see, that's where it gets complicated." Todd leaned in and whispered, "I'm the one who's pregnant."

"Oh, you're such a jerk."

"What? I can't help it." He laughed. "But no, no girlfriend for me, and no bun baking in any oven either. Plus, I haven't been with any woman ever since Hannah."

"I didn't need to know that."

"Hey you asked. But, no, I was meaning as in I've never dated anyone since her. I've been so busy with a constant work schedule that I've not really had time for a social life."

"No wonder you are back, you needed a vacation."

"Yeah, something like that."

"How long are you planning on staying?"

"That I can't be so sure. I don't know if I'm even going back." A look of despair filled his face.

"Are you sure nothing is going on?"

"Yeah, everything's fine, I promise."

She knew he was lying, but she also knew that when he was ready to talk, he would. It was then that an alarm rang out from upstairs.

Chapter Three

(2020)

5:02 A.M., Charlie Dunzy stepped in Dunzy's Coffee Shop while he turned off the security alarm. His employees didn't arrive until 5:30, he relocked the door behind him. He listened closely to hear the first batch of coffee brewing from having a timer set to go off at 5:00. Of course, the fresh aroma of the coffee told him that the first step of the day was complete.

For now, he left off the overhead lights and plugged in the icicle lights that hung around the ceiling- an idea he had from how Todd had decorated his bedroom in lights when they were kids. And then, he made his way over to the fireplace where he had a stack of wood pre-set from the night before and once they were lit, he grabbed the lonely bible from the mantel piece.

He took a seat in the leather couch across from the fireplace and skimmed to where he left off at James chapter 5. On down he read verse 13: "Is anyone among you suffering? Let him pray. Is anyone cheerful? Let him sing praise." This of course, set his mind on Todd. He knew Todd was upset the night before, but he really didn't know what of. Which, yes, that was the first time he had seen him in years, but Todd still seemed to have the whole world resting on his shoulders.

He recollected back to when he and Todd first met. Back in those days, granted they were young, Todd was the strong and fearless one...

(1995)

In a world of imagination and invisible friendships, Charlie Dunn at the age of 6, played beside his elementary school jungle gym with the *Mighty Morphin Power Ranger* action figures to keep him company. Recess was underway where kids ran around, playing, and having fun with friends. Charlie, instead, fought off Lord Zedd and his evil Putties with mostly the Green Ranger doing the fighting and leaving the rest of the Rangers to stand guard.

"Hey look, it's Chubby Charlie!" An older kid yelled out which brought Charlie out of his fantasy world. Not even Charlie's Rangers could stand against the three bullies who came his way. Each of them kicked wood chip mulch at Charlie while they taunted him in circles with, "Chubby Charlie! Chubby Charlie!"

"Leave me alone! Please!" Charlie curled up in a ball where tears rolled down his face. The Rangers lay on the ground defeated by his side while he held on tight to the Green Ranger.

"No way Chubby Charlie." One of the boys said.

"Yeah, no way, or you'll eat us." Another boy said.

"That and he'll eat the entire world!" The last boy added in. They all had a laugh, except Charlie.

"Lets help him out, huh guys? Lets give him a head start. Here Chubby Charlie, eat some dirt." One of the boys kicked dirt at Charlie's face which mixed in with his tears and left brown streaks down on his cheeks.

"Now that you all made him eat dirt, how about you guys eat some dirt as well?" A voice said behind them. One by one, each of the boys were shoved to the ground.

Charlie immediately stopped crying and watched two of the boys run away. The other boy rolled over and said, "Hey! That wasn't very nice. Why did you do that for?"

"Why do you think? You're picking on this boy here. How about you pick on somebody your own size?"

"You better watch it, or we'll beat you up too."

"Who's we? Take a look, all of your friends have left you. You are all alone. So, like I said, if you want to pick on anyone, come pick on me. I promise you, if you do, you won't be feeling happy afterwards."

The boy thought about it for a moment before he ran off as well.

"That's what I thought." The boy who saved Charlie lent out his hand. "Here, let me help you up."

Charlie came to his feet, wiped the mud and tears from his face. "Thank you."

The boy picked up the Rangers and handed them to Charlie. "It's no problem. You've just got to learn to stick up for yourself."

"I do though."

"How?"

"I just ignore them and they go away...eventually."

"Well, that doesn't seem to be helping you anymore. I've watched them pick on you for the longest time, it was about time someone did something about it."

"I'm glad. What's your name? I'm Charlie Dunzy, I mean Dunn."

"Dunzy? Todd Clinton. Nice to meet you Charlie. What grade are you in?"

"I'm in the 1st grade. You?"

"The same. Maybe we'll be in the same class next year."

"I hope so, I don't have any friends."

"I'll be your friend, Charlie."

"Really? You will?!"

"Well yeah, you seem cool to me. Power Rangers are cool. I'll bring my toys tomorrow and we can play at recess together."

"Okay!" It was the beginning of a friendship Charlie never thought would happen.

Chapter Four

(1995)

On the playground, Charlie swung back and forth on the swing set. The higher he went, the more he felt free in the wind. He felt free as if the closer he reached the sun, the closer he would be to Heaven. Even though, Heaven, wasn't a place he knew too well, but he knew it was a place where there'd be no pain and no worries. There would only be love.

The bell to end recess rang out, it was almost time for home. Then as Charlie ran into the school he noticed Todd at the water fountain. It didn't dawn on him until that moment that Todd wasn't at recess; he was so used to not having friends that it just didn't phase him, as sad as that sounds for being 6 years old. Charlie said, "Hey, Todd! Where were you? I didn't see you at recess."

"I was helping out Mr. Stooksbury in the library, I'm sorry."

"Oh...cool." Charlie stopped to catch his breath. "Hey, what are you doing after school Friday?"

"I don't know, why?"

"My mom said you could spend the night if you want to. Would you like that?" Sweat soaked Charlie's shirt.

"I'll have to ask my dad, but yes, I would like that. Sounds like it'd be fun."

"Okay! Cool! See you then!"

***

Todd ran inside his house the second he was off the school bus and immediately threw his backpack down on the couch. The channel he turned to was FOX43, and he made it just in time for the new Power Rangers episode. "Dad! Hey Dad, I'm home!"

There was no answer, and a quiet, stillness to the house.

"Dad?" He opened the side door that lead out to the garage. The car was gone. Todd thought to himself, 'Why would dad leave me home alone?'

He started to walk back to the living room when he saw a note on the fridge that said, "Hey buddy, had to run to the office real fast, will be back in just a few minutes. Lock the doors and don't answer the phones. I love you. Be good."

This was a first. He could sure take advantage of that; all the ice cream in the freezer he could eat. But wait, what if this was all a trick? What if he was secretly in hiding and waiting to see what Todd would do? Todd settled on cheese and crackers instead and then did as he was told and locked the doors. He sat down on the couch and joined in with the Rangers at Angel Grove.

When the phone rang he didn't answer: A) because he was told not to, and B) because he was too zoned in to the television. He was so zoned in that he didn't notice the shadow ease up beside him. Arms wrapped around his neck and a voice behind him said, "Arggh! A Putty has got you!"

At first, Todd screamed, but then he said, "Hi dad, I knew you were there."

"Nu-uh, why did you scream then?"

"…'cause…"

"That's right, 'cause I got you." Jim jumped over the couch and landed beside Todd. "I'm proud of you, you did exactly as I said and passed each of my tests. You're a fine young man."

"I learn from the best."

"You've got that right." He kissed Todd on the forehead. "So, what are the Rangers up against today?"

"Tommy is fighting the Green Ranger while the other Rangers have been sent back in time."

"I thought Tommy was the Green Ranger?"

"He was until he lost his powers and Zordon and Alpha turned him into the White Ranger."

"Hey, now that sounds pretty cool."

"Oh it is."

"How was your day at school?"

"It was pretty good; we are learning how to read, but you already taught me that. So I'm good there."

"See, I told you, you are smart."

"I try. Oh, you remember me telling you about my friend Charlie? He asked if I could spend the night Friday, can I go?"

"Wellll, I don't think it should be a problem. I still want to meet his parents first though."

"Okay daddy, thank you."

"You're welcome, son."

***

"Are you nervous?" Jim asked as he pulled into Charlie's driveway, where Charlie played out front with his action figures.

"A little"

"You don't have to be. Everything is going to be okay. You will have a good time. I'm really happy for you being his friend. That's what he needs right now, a good friend. You are doing the right thing."

"I just thought he seemed to be a pretty cool kid and the kids at school would not stop picking on him. I had to do something and not leave him hurt like that."

"Which, you are being a great friend for that. The Dunn family are going through a rough time. I just didn't realize who you were talking about until you mentioned his last name."

"What kind of problems are they having?"

Jim thought about it. "Well, you know how mommy isn't here with us? Their daddy isn't around the same way."

"Like, is he in heaven too?"

"No, he just...left and never came back." Charlie ran up to the car as Jim continued, "Look, don't bring that up to them- that's their business. I just want you to keep being his friend and keep being there for him. Can you do that for me?"

"Yes daddy, I can do that."

"Okay good, have a good time. I love you."

"I love you too." They hugged goodbye before Jim drove off.

***

"Hey Todd! You made it! Come on inside!" Charlie took Todd by the hand and dragged him in to the clean, but musty house of an odor of cigarette smoke. "Hey mom, Todd's here!"

Charlie's mom, Rebekkah, made her way down the stairs in both a gray sweatshirt and sweat pants. She had no makeup on with matching baggy eyes, but yet in a sweet voice to Todd, she said, "Hey there, you must be Todd. I'm Rebekkah. Charlie has told me so much about you."

"Yes, I'm Todd, that's me. Thank you for having me over." Todd's father taught him well to be a polite child.

"My pleasure. I'm glad Charlie has found himself a friend these days. If you like to, you can take your bag on up to Charlie's room and play awhile. I'm thinking of ordering a pizza, how does that sound?"

"Yay! That sounds awesome!" Both boys yelled together as they then scampered up the stairs.

As they entered Charlie's bedroom, various action figures were scattered around the shag carpet. Power Ranger posters and magazine cutouts covered the walls. And a plastic Luke Skywalker toy Lightsaber laid on the bed with the blade extended. Charlie said excitedly, "What would you like to do? I've got Legos, action figures, a Super Nintendo- anything you want!"

Todd looked around the room and his eyes landed on the Lightsaber and said, as he reached out for it, "Hey, what's this?"

"Nooo, don't touch that. A Lightsaber is to be handled carefully. It's the most dangerous weapon in the world, according to the Jedi."

"The who?"

"You've never heard of *Star Wars*!?" Charlie pushed his glasses up on his nose as his mouth hung wide open.

"No I haven't."

"Obi-Wan would be disappointed in you. You have a lot to learn. Hey! I can be your Obi-Wan and teach you the ways of the Force, and you can be my Luke!"

"Umm, okay?" Todd wasn't so sure what Charlie meant by that, but he still went along.

"Come on!" Charlie grabbed ahold of the Lightsaber and continued, "The Force is strong with that one."

The sun set in to the evening as Charlie and Todd laid on the living room floor with a half ate pizza between them, along with a large bowl of popcorn. They had already completed A New Hope, and were now on the Empire Strikes Back. Luke and Vader were battling it out on the screen when Todd glanced over at the dining room where Rebekkah sipped on tea and read through bills scattered on the table. In his eyes she looked like a strong and hard working mother, much like his father. She looked like someone who had everything in control with what the world around her threw out. Yet, what he didn't understand, was that underneath her smile, stress clung on as tight as possible.

Todd daydreamed of what it would like to have a mother such as her, or better yet, a mother at all. Which, the daydream was interrupted by an oncoming car with music that blared so loud it rattled the windows. As the car pulled in to the driveway, it shined bright lights through the edges of the closed curtains.

"Oh no, Lord Zedd and his repulsive girlfriend, Rita, and their putty goons are home." The happy smile from Charlie's face faded in that instant. He clinched on to the Lightsaber to the point that white shown on his knuckles.

Before Todd could even ask who Charlie talked about, the front door burst open by a skinny guy with long brown hair. The skinny guy had his arm around a girl with spike green hair. And then behind them followed four other guys who were dressed in all black and had multi colored hair. One of the guys yelled out, "Pizza! Righteous!" before he scurried up the box. What was left of the pizza was devoured in nearly seconds.

"Hey there little brother, how's it going?" The skinny guy said as he let his arm fall from the girl's shoulder and punched Charlie in the arm.

"Owww!" Charlie screamed.

"Oh come on! I didn't hit you that hard, you big baby!"

Rebekkah came into the room and looked at the skinny guy and said, "Brad, fellas, not tonight. We've got a guest over."

"I'm just playing with him mom, chill out." Brad said.

Charlie gripped the Lightsaber even tighter.

"I don't care if you are playing," Rebekkah continued, "I just think it's best if you guys don't stay here tonight."

"Actually, as a matter of fact, I'm 18 and have say so if my friends can stay or not. I can do as I please." Brad said.

"Yes, and no. You live under my roof, Bradly, you obey my rules. If you start helping out on these bills then it would be an entirely different story. Until then, your friends need to go."

"Fine then, have it your way." Brad headed to the front door and continued, "Come on fellas, lets get out of here. I don't need this tonight."

"Brad, please," Rebekkah said, "just think about what you're doing. I can tell you right now, it won't be easy out there. Here, though, you have food, clothes, and a roof over your head- you've got it made. The second you leave, you'll lose it all. Don't be like this."

"Don't be like what? Dad? Or better yet, the *man* who left his wife and kids to fend for themselves? Or no, wait, it all makes sense to me now- he didn't leave you, you pushed him away just like you are pushing me away now. If things don't go mom's way she will just kick them to the curb. Real mature mom, real mature."

Rebekkah was stunned. "Brad...I..."

"That's what I thought. Lets go." Brad opened the door.

On the way out, one of Brad's friends, Ricky, kicked over the popcorn bowl and said, "Oops, sorry kid."

Sure, it got a laugh from all the friends, but it was all Charlie could take; that was the last time anyone would pick on him, and the last time anyone would make his mother cry. He was up in an instant as he screamed at the top of his lungs. Something inside of him snapped, there was nothing stopping him, he ran through the group of friends and ran straight to his brother.

"Whoa! Whoa! Ow! Ow! Hey- stop! Stop!" Brad screamed with every whack of the plastic Lightsaber. Charlie wouldn't let up and envisioned each and every hit as a way of revenge for every cruel moment from bullies at school and bullying from his brother as well.

"Stop it! You're hurting him!" Brad's girlfriend, Jill screamed. She too, was afraid to go near Charlie who had Brad pinned up against his car. Brad was terrified, he hadn't seen his brother like this before. It took all of his friends to pull Charlie away, all the while as they dodged the swings from getting hit themselves.

Charlie dropped his Lightsaber and collapsed in Rebekka's arms, out of breath and cheeks soaked with tears.

Brad took a step toward him, but Jill put her hand on his chest and said, "No Brad, just leave it. Lets go, huh? Forget this place, they aren't worth your time."

Bloodied and bruised, Brad's hands shook as he lit a cigarette. All he could say was, "Yeah."

Nothing else was said. They all drove off leaving Charlie, Todd, and Rebekkah on the front lawn.

Chapter Five

(1995)

They drove in silence as Brad chain smoked the entire way. Nobody wanted to irritate him any more than he already was. Jill placed her hand on his leg, even though he never acknowledged it was there. What a night this had turned out to be.

Where they ended up was at a cabin of which they'd spend many weekends partying. Brad's friends got out of the car first and he sat alone with his thoughts. Each thought only intensified his anger. He decided on having a drink. One beer lead to another as the night went on.

His friends (Ricky, Logan, Stan, and Derek) all challenged each other to a game of pool. Brad sat in a maroon leather chair with Jill on his lap and her arms wrapped around his neck. His eyes were locked on a half empty bottle of beer in his hand. He barely said a word the entire night. All he wanted to do was mellow out, let loose and have fun, but the earlier event only kept circling around in his mind.

"Get off me Jill, I can't do this right now." He picked her up like a feather and sat her back down in the chair.

"Geeze, I'm sorry." She snorted.

"Don't start with me Jill, I'm not in the mood." Brad replied.

"Pfft, whatever. Like you are the only one with problems."

"Well at least I don't pretend to love my boyfriend while I'm sleeping around behind his back with his friend, oh lets see, Ricky." Brad tensed up.

Ricky was concentrated hard on the 8 ball when heard his name and flinched. He scratched and lost the game. He said, "Whoa! Hey, that's not true. I'd never do that to you, Brad. You're my boy."

"Tell me another one, why don't you?" Brad chugged the rest of his beer and glanced at the empty bottle and smashed it against the wall. "I'm just so sick of everyone! There's nobody I can trust. Everyone *always* seems to either stab me in the back or leaves me when I need them the most. I'm surprised any of you all are still around."

Logan grabbed a broom and dust pan to clean up the glass and said, "We love you man, that's why. We aint going anywhere, I promise."

"Oh really? That's the same exact little speech my dad gave me when he was leaving. I never saw him again." Brad said.

"My dad left also, I know how you feel. It does get better, trust me." Logan assured him.

"No," Brad said, "it doesn't get better, and it never will. My mom's right, I have *nothing*. This is it for me."

"Baby, please, come sit back down with me. You have me, I'm all you need." Jill pleaded.

"What and move in with you and your insane sisters and their drug fiend boyfriends? No thank you. I'll figure something out, just- ugh, if it wasn't for my dad I wouldn't be in this situation right now. I promise you, that if I was to ever find him, he won't be living in the morning."

"Come on man, don't say that." Stan cut in.

"Why not, Stan? You surely don't know how I feel; how empty I am. All I want to do is get on with my life, but

I can't. I just don't get how my brother and so-called mother can live so happy knowing what that man left us with. It's so messed up."

"Yeah! That woman hates me. Forget her. She doesn't realize how-" Jill hiccupped and continued, "how amazing her son is. All she cares about is her baby and herself. She pushed you away, what's up with that?"

Derek stuck his head around the side of the fridge, "Hey, uh, we're out of beer."

"Oh great, more to worry about." Brad grabbed his car keys. "I'll go get the beers and I'll take care of everyone's problems."

Logan stepped in between Brad and the door as quick as he could and said, "Listen, Brad, just wait awhile. You've been drinking, you don't need this right now."

"Logan, I love you man, but you best be getting out of my way. You're right, I don't need this, it's not even the time to play hero with me either. Whatever happens to me tonight I could care less. I just have to get out of here. Now, if you would, kindly step away from the door before this gets ugly."

He admitted defeat and Logan sighed as he stepped away from the door with his head down. He couldn't even look at Brad in the eyes as he walked out into the night.

Chapter Six

(1995)

In the late hours of the night, gas station clerk named Bill stood behind the counter as he counted boxes of cigarettes to pass the time. It was dead quiet, which at this hour there was hardly any customers, except for the occasional truck driver. Then again, there were times he had to deal with homeless people scrounging through trash cans, but that was the life Bill Dunzy chose to live as a gas station clerk.

Bill turned around as someone walked in the front door. "Good eve-" he tried to say, but recognized the customer on the first glance, a shadow of his former self.

Bradly walked on by without saying a word and went straight to the coolers. He barely even gave Bill eye contact as he walked up to the counter with two six packs in his hands.

"Will this be all for you?" Bill asked.

Bradly reached in his jacket pocket and pulled out a pack of cigarettes and checked to see how many he had left before he returned them to his pocket. Still no eye contact and said, "No, that'll be it."

"I'd have to see your ID." Even though Bill knew who he was, he kept going to see if Bradly would notice him as well.

Bradly was already frustrated enough but shook his head as he handed Bill his wallet. It didn't help that Bill burst in to laughter. "What? What's so funny?" It was then that Bradly recognized who the clerk was. His eyes went wide and he continued, "Oh, it's you. Look, if you don't mind, I'd just like to get out of here. Now, would you please ring me up and lets get this over with?"

"Sorry, but I can't. And just curious, when did you turn into a twenty-eight year old Chinese man?"

"Since when did you become a man and get a job?"

"Brad-"

"No!" Brad cut him off. "No! Don't, Brad, me. You have no idea how pissed off I am, and you're in the wrong place at the wrong time, *dad*."

"I'm sorry, Brad, I know you're hurt. It's been years since I've seen you. I didn't expect us to meet up like this."

"Three-" Brad punched the counter. He took a deep breath, grabbed one of the beers, twisted off the cap and tossed it behind him. With a quick chug, he belched.

"Feel better?"

"I'm just getting started."

"You're what, 16, 17 now and already drinking and smoking? I was just like you at your age."

"Why do you care anyways? As far as I'm concerned, you left us in the cold. And plus, I learned the bad habits from you. According to mom, yes, I'm just like you. And for the record, I'm 18, thank you very much."

"My, my, 18." Bill leaned against the wall and crossed his arms. "Son, you really don't know what your mother and I went through. Yeah, I drank, but it was only a little, maybe once every other week. Your mother has some really bad emotional issues."

"That's really so hard to believe. And what, so you just said, 'forget it' and leave your teenage son and toddler alone if she was that "emotionally distressed"? Oh yeah, that's really a father figure there. So, are you happy then? Are you happy working *here* and happy the way your son turned out?"

"I'm not happy at all." Bill wiped away the tears that formed in his eyes. "How are you doing these days?"

"Wow, really? How am *I* doing? How. Am. I. Doing?" Brad clenched the empty beer bottle. "Yeah, that's right, cry. Cry, you big baby for leaving your family behind. Cry for your oldest son who has nowhere to go, while your wife sits at home with hardly anything to her name, who struggles to get by. And while you're at it, cry for your youngest son who gets the crap beat out of him at school because he's so shy and chubby, but he's such a smart kid. He certainly doesn't have a father figure in his life, that's for sure. So, cry..."

Bradly heaved the bottle at Bill where he had to duck not to get hit. It smashed on the wall where his head would've been.

"Cry..."

He tossed another bottle, this time one that was full.

"Cry..."

Bill dodged every bottle except for the last one that skimmed his ear. He grabbed ahold of the other six pack before Bradly could get a hold of it. Bradly leapt the counter instead and landed on top of Bill and wailed on him.

At that very moment, Officer O'Reilley stepped inside and began to say, "Evening, Bill, fresh pot of coffee for-" But, he instead saw the commotion on the floor behind the counter and ran to Bill's aide.

Chapter Seven

(1995)

After Charlie had collapsed in Rebekkah's arms, she fell to her knees on the front lawn. She tried everything she could to wake him, but nothing would work. So, she carried him inside, laid him on the couch and ran to the kitchen.

Todd got down on his knees beside Charlie and spoke softly to him, "Hey buddy, I'm here. Nobody is going to hurt you, I promise. It's just me and our mom. Can you wake up, please?"

"Hmph, mommy, I don't want to go to school." Charlie moaned.

"Me neither, but I'm not mommy, I'm Todd."

"Todd?"

"Yeah, buddy. It's me."

"Whe-where am I?"

"Your couch."

"What happened?"

"You defeated Zedd with your Lightsaber and fell asleep."

"Wow, I did?" With Charlie's eyes closed he still smiled the biggest smile.

"Yes, you did. You stood up to him. You're a real Jedi now."

"Awesome." He opened his eyes and looked over at Todd and said, "Thank you for being here with me. I couldn't have done it without you."

Rebekkah froze in the doorway with a damp washcloth in her hands and said, "Charlie? My baby! You're awake!"

Todd moved out of the way just in time for Rebekkah to scoop up Charlie in her arms.

"I'm okay, mommy." Charlie said. "Really, I'm okay. Are you mad at me for hurting Brad?"

"No baby, not at all. I'm so happy you are okay. I was so scared." She held him close and bawled.

"Mommy, why are you crying?"

"I'm just happy that you are okay. I thought you were really hurt."

Todd picked up a cup of Pepsi and tapped Rebekkah on the shoulder. She gave it to Charlie and then said to Todd, "Thank you Todd, that's really sweet of you. I'm so sorry you had to see all of this tonight. Come on Charlie, lets go get you cleaned up."

They were only gone for a few minutes, but in the meantime, Todd cleaned up the mess in the living room made by Brad and his friends. He didn't have to, but Todd felt it was the generous thing to do; he just loved to help his father, so it all has come naturally to him.

When Rebekkah and Charlie came back down stairs she suggested, "Hey, why don't you guys finish watching

Empire and I'll make a new batch of popcorn? Then after that we could watch Return of the Jedi. Sound good?"

Charlie was dressed in his pajamas by now and ready for the sleep over adventures to continue. They were all up for the continuation of the *Star Wars* marathon, but as Jedi came to a close the two boy's snores synchronized in with the film. Rebekkah turned off the movie and covered them up while they slept on the floor. She kissed Charlie on the forehead and headed back to the kitchen.

***

Hours later, the boys were woken up by a deep, but calm voice that said, "Boys, hey boys, time to wake up."

The bedroom light was on and when Charlie opened his eyes he didn't recognize the man at all, but yet, Todd knew him and said, "Dad? What are you doing here? Are you spending the night too? You might want to ask Charlie's mom first."

Jim chuckled, "No, no. I need you boys to come with me, we're going to our house."

"Where's my mommy?" Charlie asked as he pulled himself up and noticed blue lights flashing outside the window. "Is everything okay? Please, where's my mommy?"

Jim had no clue how to approach the boy, certainly not knowing how he'd react. When he had to break the news to Todd about his mother's passing, he was a lot younger than Charlie. Only, Charlie's mother did not pass. He said, "She's going to be okay, she's just really sick. We will talk more about it when we get to our house, okay?"

Unsure of what to believe, Charlie still had Todd by his side and Todd would protect him no matter what and so he said, "Okay, can I take my Lightsaber?"

"Of course you can," Jim answered.

Jim followed behind the boys as they stepped out in the cool night still in their pajamas, backpacks strapped over their shoulders. Charlie's green Lightsaber lead the way through rows of police cars and a police detective talking to neighbors. Officer O'Reilley followed behind Jim until they got to his house and when they got there he shook Jim's hand and said, "Thanks again for this."

"It's really no problem at all. I hope you find her, and that everything is just fine."

"Oh I'm sure it will be, we've got a control on everything. Have a good night."

Officer O'Reilley climbed back in his car and as he drove off, Charlie happened to look up and see Brad asleep in the backseat with his head rested against the window. He cried out, "Hey! That's my brother! What's going on?"

***

When he arrived at the Precent, Officer O'Reilley sat down with Detective Windell. It had been a long night, they were both relieved to enjoy a cup of coffee. Windell said, "Okay, lets start from the beginning. Tell me what happened."

Officer O'Reilley began with the arrest of Brad Dunn and then said, "Bill didn't want to press charges, he blamed himself for Brad's actions. So, I drove him home and by the time I got there he was passed out in the backseat of the cruiser. I didn't want to just leave him there, so I went to see if Rebekkah was home. She opened the door almost immediately and politely welcomed me in. There was a glass of wine in her hand and I noticed both boys sound asleep on the living room floor, nothing unusual with that.

I then told her what was wrong, how Brad had assaulted her husband and was passed out in the cruiser. The color of her face drained and I was for sure she was going to pass out right then and there, but she instead went quiet and walked to the kitchen. I waited for a moment until I heard glass shatter. I ran to her, but she was nowhere to be found with the back door wide open. Her glass was shattered on the floor and the bottle over turned on the counter with the wine spilling over.

When I stepped outside, she was nowhere to be seen or heard. It was then I called for back-up. And, so, not to cause any more commotion, I saw that one of the boys was Jim Clinton's son, so I called him and informed him of the situation. It wasn't long until you all arrived."

Detective Windell rubbed his cheek in thought and said, "The only thing we can do is find her."

Chapter Eight

(1995)

Charlie bawled most of the night, but Todd knew how it felt to have his world turned upside down and just held him close. He unfortunately knew, that even at their young age, that things were going to get worse before they would even get better.

Jim had carried Charlie in to the house and sat him down on the couch and proceeded to calm him down, "Charlie, hey buddy, shh, shh, shh it's okay. Everything is going to be okay, I promise. Hey, how about some hot chocolate? Would you boys like that? Extra marshmallows on the house."

"Ye-" Charlie sniffled, "Yeah."

His crying slowed down some as he watched Jim in the kitchen making the drink. To him, it was certainly a different sight than to see his mother in the kitchen. He couldn't help but wonder if this was how real daddies were.

"Here you go man, you dropped this." Todd handed Charlie his Lightsaber.

"Thanks!" Charlie held it close to him as if it were his teddy bear. "This saved my life today."

Jim came in and handed each boy a mug of hot chocolate and he asked Charlie, "You really have had a rough day, haven't you? Would you like to talk about it?"

"I just don't understand what's going on. Where's my mommy? Why is my brother in the police car? Nothing makes any sense to me."

"Well...God has a reason for everything. He's with us even when we least expect it. I don't know for sure what your brother did, but God is giving him a chance to better himself. From what I've heard is that he's been in a lot of trouble, so now he can get some help. And now, your mommy is just lost somewhere, but they are going to find her."

Charlie sat back and took it all in. His crying was over, but he just wanted things to be over and back to the way they were.

"I tell you what," Jim continued, "I see that you have a Lightsaber there, why don't we watch the *Star Wars* movies?"

"I don't want to right now." Charlie lowered his head and looked down at his feet. "I'm sorry."

"It's perfectly alright." Jim glanced at Todd who had a look of confusion on his face of what to do. He said, "Hey Todd, do you still have your Power Ranger costumes?"

Todd and Charlie dressed in the red and blue Power Ranger costumes, fought off the evil Jimmony monster in through the early Saturday morning hours. The trick had helped- Charlie's mind was free of the chaos the night before, and now, he smiled and laughed more than he had in a long time. For once, his little life had not a single worry.

By that afternoon, Rebekkah had still not been found, nor any word on what was becoming of Brad either. The boys spent their day, after the Jimmony monster was destroyed, playing video games. Jim now worried himself about the future ahead for Charlie. He watched the boys from his recliner, with a cup of coffee in his hand, and waited by his phone for any call. When the phone did ring, he answered it on the first ring and said, "Officer O'Reilley? How is-"

Charlie dropped his controller and turned to face Jim.

***

The police had combed the area all night looking for Rebekkah Dunn. No trace of her could be found, until miles down the road, an anonymous caller reported a strange lady walking down the road wearing a trash bag like a dress. An officer near the area made the first response, drove down the road and ended up passing her by. She didn't make an acknowledgment of his presence. Her distant eyes were locked straight ahead, in a different world all together.

He made a U-turn, pulled up in front of her and stepped out of his vehicle. "Mrs. Rebekkah Dunn, is everything okay?"

She made no response.

"Ma'am, my name is Peter. Can I help you with anything?"

Slowly, she turned her head to face him and said, "Peter?"

"Yes ma'am- Peter."

"Are you here to help slay the dragons too?"

"I'm sorry?"

"The dragons. Are you here to slay them too? My son slayed a dragon earlier today. I'm so proud of him. He's a prince, you know? And one day, he'll be a king and protect this kingdom."

"That's very good ma'am. I can't help with the dragons, but I tell you what, I can give you a ride in my carriage to the castle. We can talk to somebody there about slaying the dragons. How does that sound?"

Smiled real big and said, "That sounds like a great plan to me."

***

Jim kept his eyes on Charlie and replied to the voice over the phone, "Great! That's just great! Oh, she's where? Oh my, that's not good. Well, can't he just stay here until...I see...okay, I understand."

He hung up the phone and sighed. Charlie knew that look of disappointment on Jim's face and said, "It's my mom, isn't it?"

At that moment, Jim didn't see Charlie as a little boy any longer, he looked like a strong young man. He knew he couldn't lie to him, "Yeah Charlie, your mommy's...sick and is in a special hospital right now. There's going to be someone come pick you up in a little while and take you somewhere."

"No! I want to stay here with you! I want to stay here with Todd and play! This is no fair at all!" Charlie said and ran and jumped in Jim's arms. He hugged him tight and bawled.

"Hey, hey, hey, Charlie, it's okay. Shh, listen- hey, listen." Jim tried to be as calm as he could, "I'm sorry all of this is going on. You are going through so much right now, but I want you to know that it's not your fault. None of it is. You are a wonderful kid, Charlie Dunn. God will always be with you."

"Will He?"

"Of course He will. All He wants is for you to be strong, courageous, and love Him. Can you do that? Can you do that for me?"

"Sure, sure I can."

Not long after than when Charlie was being picked up with his *Star Wars* backpack on his shoulders he turned around and asked Todd, "Will I ever see you again?"

"Yes you will. We will always be friends, I promise you that, Charlie Dunzy." Todd said.

He wasn't sure where he was headed, or sure of what the future held, but just knowing Charlie had friends out there who cared for him that much, he knew he was going to be okay and smiled through the pain.

Chapter Nine

(2001)

Todd checked his hair in the mirror- he had way too much gel, but he had to be cool for his first day of Junior High. He had on baggy jeans and a *Star Wars* Episode 1 t-shirt and black and white Converse shoes- ready to go.

"Todd! For the umpteenth time!" Jim yelled from the bottom of the stairs.

"Coming!"

Todd ran down to the kitchen and sat next to a Jim who had hair that was now grey. They were both just about the same height. Jim turned to Todd and said, "Whew! Boy! How much of that gel did you use?"

"Not a whole lot."

"Not a whole lot? That's not hair, that's concrete on top of your head. No wonder you couldn't hear me, you've probably got cement in your ears as well."

"Sorry, I'm just trying to make myself look flyyy." Todd flipped the neck of his collar.

It took everything for Jim to keep a straight face and not burst in to laughter. He said, "Real smooth, Todd, real smooth."

"Maaan, you know it. Sugar Bear's got to be there for the ladies."

"Umm."

"You dig?"

"Someone better just be digging into those eggs so that someone could be digging into this work is all I can say. You dig?"

"Yeah, yeah, Pops. I dig."

"Right on son, right on." They both laughed. "Oh you're making me feel old."

"Psh, I think that hair of yours has a little something to do with that. You look like a Dalmatian with all of those gray spots."

"Wow."

"Hey, it aint nothing but a chicken wing."

"Alright, alright. Seriously, Todd, I'm proud of you. You're growing into a fine young man- Junior High now, and soon will be a teenager."

"What do you mean *growing*? Man, I'm already *fine*."

"Well, you certainly have that teenage cockiness for sure."

"Word."

***

He *was* confident, and he *was* cool...until he stepped off the school bus and saw just how small he was compared to the 7th and 8th graders. The year before, in 5th grade, the teachers lead him on how much older and wiser they were all going to be in Junior High- how much larger of a world they would be entering into. What they had failed to mention, was that they'd be starting out on bottom. It was like Kindergarten all over again.

All of the 6th graders had a mandatory assembly on the first day of school before letting the young'uns run free throughout the school. The auditorium was dimly lit that had wooden stadium seats that were obviously older than even their parents were, and the walls were covered with a red fabric like a huge curtain. The place, mixed in with the old musty smell, was kind of creepy really- the dungeon of Halls Middle School.

Todd walked in and didn't expect to see as many 6th graders as he did. There had to be hundreds of them, or at least that's what it looked like to him. All of them conversed with one another, their high-pitched voices loud and unnerving. He sat in the back, not really wanting to mingle with anyone just yet.

The door behind him slammed open and a group of boys sat at the other end of the row. One of the boys was obviously annoyed with the other as he said, "What?! You've got to be kidding me?? Sure, okay, *Star Trek* is good and all, but it doesn't even compare to the awesomeness of *Star Wars*!"

As much as Todd didn't want to mingle, this was his cue that he had to cut in. "Okay," he said as he walked down the aisle, "I have to agree, *Star Wars* is way better."

"Thank you! I'm-" the aggravated boy stopped talking in midsentence and locked eyes with Todd. "Todd? No way! Is that you?"

"No way! Charlie Dunzy!" They both embraced in a hug after so many years apart. "How've you been? I never thought I'd ever see you again."

Charlie looked the same as he did in the past, minus some of the weight he had. And of course, he wore a similar *Star Wars* t-shirt. On top of that, he wore a silver cross around his neck.

"I've been great, living with foster parents who love me to pieces. You can only imagine what has gone on since we last saw each other. That was a pretty bad night, huh? How about you? How've you been?"

"I've been good. It's still just my dad and I. And, because of you, I'm addicted to *Star Wars*. So, the Clinton home is a *Star Wars* home now." Todd chuckled.

"Hey, can't beat that. How is your dad doing? You know, he really inspired me that night. And so did you. You both made such a wonderful impact on my life that I've given my life to God. Which, having a Christian foster family really helped out huge as well."

"Charlie, that's really amazing! How did we do that? And dad's strong and crazy as ever, 'cause he's in denial about being old, but still. He's just crazy."

"That's a dad for you though. And in just that short time I was there, he showed me what a REAL dad should be- lovable and caring, unlike my own dad who wasn't around at the time. He taught me about God; and then with you, you taught me how to stick up for myself and just be ME. It was all God bringing us together for a purpose."

"Wow...I'm touched, Charlie. I just thought you were a cool kid and needed a friend. And given everything that happened, you seem happy to me."

"Todd, I am..I'm really happy, you have no idea. Granted, yes, that night I lost everything; my mom went insane and is in a mental institution, and my brother is in jail for who knows how long, but I have a whole new life and a life with Christ. I have no reason to be bitter about my past, because in the present and the future, there is grace."

"Are you sure you're only 12? You just completely blew me away. I could've swore you were an adult in a child's body."

"Hey, people like you and I, who have pretty much grew up depending on ourselves tend to mature a lot quicker than others. Buddy, we have two qualities that's pretty amazing: we have God, and we have...the Force."

Todd laughed, "Isn't that the truth."

Their conversation was cut short with the start of the assembly. To the boy's surprise, they had almost every class together. This was going to be a great first year in Junior High.

At the end of the day as they walked out of the school, Todd headed toward the busses as Charlie headed toward the visitor parking. Charlie turned around and said to Todd, "Hey Todd! We should hang out again sometime; now that we know we are friends again."

"Yeah we definitely should! Where do you live anyways? I was wondering how all of a sudden we are going to the same school, but didn't go to the same elementary school."

"I think it's cause of the Knox County school zone differences. I only moved a few streets from my old house...which is an odd feeling when we'd pass by it and knowing I don't live there anymore."

"Oh yeah, I can imagine. And that's so odd, that even still, we lived that close to each other and yet never seen each other in the past 6 years."

"Hey, well, we both know that God has a perfect timing and plan for all of us." Charlie said as he turned and walked away.

Chapter Ten

(2001)

"Good morning man!" Todd greeted Charlie as he watched him walk into class.

"Dude, you won't believe this!" Charlie said.

"Two seconds." Todd finished reading the chapter he was on, marked his page, and closed the book. "Sorry, I'm weird when I read, I can't just stop where I'm at. I have to finish a chapter."

"And I thought I had problems."

Todd gave him a stern look.

"I'm only kidding," Charlie said. "So, get this- I've been reading up on it, and *Star Wars* Episode 2 comes out this year! Man, I can't wait!"

"Oh I know! It's going to…to…" Todd faded out. His eyes wouldn't leave the girl that just walked into the room.

"Todd, you okay?…Todd…Earth to Todd…What are you-?" Charlie turned in his seat to see what Todd glared at. The girl was new and handed her class list to the teacher to make sure she had the right room. "Oh, I see…it's our Leia."

"…Leia…" Todd whispered.

"Todd!" Charlie snapped. He grabbed Todd's book and hit him over the head with it.

"Oww! What?"

"Zone back in, man."

"I'm here."

"Yeah, sure you are." Charlie smirked.

"I was!"

"Okay, what was we talking about?"

"*Star Wars.*"

"Okay, what about it?"

Todd thought for a second, then said, "Leia?"

BONK Charlie hit him again then pointed to the new girl. "No, THAT's Leia. We were talking about Episode 2."

"Oh, sorry, man."

"No worries, it was funny though. Your eyes were bugged out of your head."

"Were they really?"

"Umm, yeahhh."

"That's funny." Todd grabbed his book. "So, explain how she is Leia."

"It's a metaphor, meaning you and I are like Luke and Han and she walked in and so she's Leia."

"Oh." Todd sat in silence for a moment while Charlie got his books together. "Hey, wouldn't it really be I'm Luke and you're Obi-Wan since it was *you* who introduced me to the Wars?"

"Ha, good point." Charlie said.

The new girl started to walk toward them. Todd could feel the perspiration roll down his back. He tried to play it cool and opened his book. She looked at him with a smile and said, "Hi."

Todd didn't think about what he said, just said, "Leia...I mean."

"What?" She asked, confused.

"He means, 'hi'." Charlie laughed and stuck out his hand. "I'm Charlie Dunzy."

She shook his hand and said, "Dunzy? I'm Hannah Napp."

"Nice to meet you, and this is my good friend, Todd Clinton who gave me the Dunzy nick-name."

Hannah held out her hand to Todd and said, "Hello there."

"Howdy." Todd smiled and shook her hand.

"Is this seat taken?" She pointed to the seat in front of Todd. He shook his head and she smiled as she sat down. She turned around to Todd and said, "Nice book, by the way."

Charlie laughed as she turned back around. Both he and Todd noticed that the book Todd held was upside down the entire time. Charlie whispered to Todd, "And I thought I was the shy one."

Chapter Eleven

(2001)

"So when's this friend of yours supposed to be coming over?" Jim asked Todd as he straightened up the living room.

"Here shortly. Don't worry, I know you'll like him."

"Knowing you, that worries me. And the fact I know how you teenagers change your mind every other day on who you are and what trend is in. So, yes, it's frightening not knowing whom you'll be bringing home."

"Hey, at least I'm not bringing a girl to stay over the weekend. Although..."

"Don't even think about it. I trust you, but I'm not going that far. I was a boy once before, I know how you think."

"Soooo, you aren't a boy now? I knew there was something funny about you."

"Ohh, you lit-" Jim was about to say when a knock came from the front door.

"Ha! Saved by the bell."

Jim smacked Todd with a pillow as he walked by. Todd opened the door and said, "Hey man, come on in. I'm surprised you still remember the place."

"It wasn't hard to find." Charlie said as he stepped inside.

"My word..." Jim stopped. "Charlie Dunn."

"In the flesh. How's it going old man?"

"I'm good...I..." Jim began.

"Uh oh, he's about to cry." Todd explained.

"Sorry," Jim continued, "Come here and give me a hug. It's so good to see you. Are you doing well?"

"Yeah, yeah, I'm doing great, to be honest. Like I told Todd, I'm not the least bit bitter of the past. It was all a part of God's plan. He was there for me like you said."

"You remember that?" Jim asked.

"Of course. It was my first lesson about God, and it stuck with me. Which, Jim, I want to thank you for being there for me back then. You were more of a father for me than my own dad."

Jim wiped the tears from his eyes and said, "No need to thank me, that was all God looking out for you. I knew how hard it was to lose someone, so my heart felt for you as my own son. We would've welcomed you in our home if the courts would've let us, but because of it being just Todd and I they didn't see it fit."

"There's no worries at all- I completely understand that, which I'm fine. I think I turned out okay. And just think, 6 years later here I am again."

"Which, lets make sure *this* time that nothing bad happens." Todd added.

They all ordered pizza and spent the night playing video games. Jim played along and tried his hardest to understand the game, but he still had fun regardless.

***

The next morning, the boys slept in and woke late. Charlie said as he sat up and still tried to wake up, "So, what do you want to do today? Last night was the most fun I've had in a long time."

"I'm not really sure yet. Usually dad and I go to McArthur's Used Book store on the weekends, but if that's something you wouldn't want to do is fine with me.

"That sounds like a good idea to me! Lets go!"

Jim dropped them off while he went and ran errands. The first section they went to was the Recently Added books. Todd said, "Feel free to look anywhere you like; they've got all kinds of books, as well as cd's, movies, and games. It's a nerd Heaven."

"I can't believe I've never been here before. You learn something new every day." Charlie said.

"It's basically my second home."

"I can't complain about that, there's a certain warmth and smell here that's relaxing to the soul." Charlie said as he took in the atmosphere.

"You must be smelling the coffee from Pedal Java outside, or maybe the old books. Either way, I agree. Do you drink coffee?"

"No, I've never had it. Is it any good?"

"It's delicious, especially the Milky Way frappe. Everyone I know drinks it like crazy."

"Hmm, I may have to give it a shot today." Charlie pondered.

The boys took their time as they walked around- many books to choose from. Charlie was amazed at how cheap the books were, how they were half the price (if not more than that) than a retail book store. As they made their way around to the Christian book section, Todd stopped to miss running into a lady. He said, "Excuse me, I'm so-."

"Do you ever finish a sentence around me? Todd, right?" Hannah laughed. She turned to Charlie and said, "Fancy running into you guys."

"It was nice running into you too." Charlie glanced over at Todd who practically drooled. "I'm going to try that coffee shop, you kids be good."

Charlie patted Todd on the back as he let his nose guide him to the coffee.

"Coffee does sound good, I could go for a cup of Joe. How about you?" Hannah asked Todd. Of course, he agreed to the invitation.

After the barista, Andy, asked what he could get Charlie, Charlie wasn't so sure. He stood and studied the menu, that of which everything had a name he couldn't pronounce and was all like a foreign language to him. "I've never had coffee before, what would you choose?" He asked Andy who leaned against his bicycle as he wore his favorite vest.

"Hmm, well, lets see..." Andy thought about it, "How about I give you a sample of everything and then you can decide on what's your favorite?"

"Deal. Hit me up Jeeves." Charlie said in a fancy British voice.

"Is this spot okay?" Todd asked as he suggested a booth by the window.

"Perfect choice." Hannah scooted on in.

Todd sat across from her and slid his books to the side. He had no idea what he was going to talk about, and he was certain she could sense how nervous he was. She broke the ice and said, "So, given the obvious, you like reading huh?"

"I love it. It's one of my favorite hobbies. What about you? Well, that might explain why you're in a book store." He thought to himself, *'Okay, easy enough.'*

"Ha, yeah that does explain it. I do love to read- I read more than anyone in my family. And Todd..." She placed her hand on top of his, cautiously not to give him a heart attack and continued, "Don't be nervous. I'm no one special for someone to be nervous over. I'm just another girl."

Not even thinking about it, he said the first thing that came to his lips, "Yeah, but, you are just the most beautiful girl I've ever seen. I'm not really used to talking to girls. Period. I just freeze up. This is the most I've ever said to a girl."

"You're doing just fine to me. I know when you do open up, you'll be a great friend."

"Thank you. What makes you think I'll be a great friend?"

"I've seen you and Charlie around school together. You both are so funny and sweethearts."

"Charlie brings that out of me. We're just crazy nerds is all. He introduced me to *Star Wars*, and I took up for him when the other kids put him down."

"See, I told you, you are a sweetheart. I take it you and he have been friends for a long time?"

"Um, yes and no. We met in elementary school, but because of certain family circumstances I haven't seen him in years. We just never forgot each other."

"That's a true friendship right there."

"Yeah, he's like a brother to me." Todd said.

Charlie ran over to them, shaking all over. He said, "Dude! Dude! Dude! You've got to try these drinks, they are amazing! Hi Hannah!" He looked back and forth between the two. "Todd, I absolutely love coffee! Man I can't sit still. I feel so free!"

It was then that Charlie ran out of the store.

"Well that was different." Hannah laughed.

"There's a first for everything." Todd said.

"It's great you and him are so close. Back at my old school I didn't really have any friends like that. Well, I don't here either, but that's beside the point."

"Well hey, you are more than welcome to hang out with Charlie and me. He won't mind."

"Really?" Hannah smiled, for the first time she felt accepted.

"Of course." Todd smiled back. He mainly let the butterflies in his stomach guide his movements.

Charlie ran by the window chasing a bird and screamed, "Here birdie, birdie, birdie, birdie!"

"Do you think we need to go get him?" Hannah asked.

"I think we should, but I kind of want to see how this will play out. There's no telling what he will do."

"I can't stay out much longer, I told my mom I'd only be gone a little while. I'm still getting used to the town."

"Did you walk here?"

"No, I rode my bike. Would you like to walk me out?" They both walked out and Hannah continued, "Hey, where's Charlie?"

He wasn't anywhere in sight, nor could he be seen. "I have noooo idea," Todd said. "Oh wait, never mind...I see him."

Charlie was at the other end of the parking lot, leaping head first in to the bushes.

"Yeahh, you better go get him," Hannah suggested. "It was great talking to you."

"Oh, you too. Hey, uh, can I give you a call sometime?" Todd asked.

"Well sure." They exchanged numbers and Hannah said, "See you Todd."

Todd watched her roll away before he went after Charlie- who now sang a rendition of 'I'm a little tea pot'. You'd think he was drunk, but nope...just coffee- many, many different varieties of coffee from the world famous Pedal Java.

Chapter Twelve

(2001)

"So, what's this surprise you wanted to show me?" Todd asked as Charlie came over on another weekend.

Charlie unzipped his backpack, reached inside and pulled out a green Lightsaber. "Check it out."

"No way!" Todd yelled, "Is that *the* Lightsaber?"

"The one and only." Charlie smiled. "And if you look closely, you can still see scuff marks from Brad's face."

"Wow, that's really awesome. I'm shocked you still have it after all these years."

"Yeah, well, it's just one possession I can't live without. It saved my life and so it'll never leave my side. I plan on being buried with it."

"No joke?" Todd asked.

"No joke. And you know what's even better?" Charlie reached in his bag again and pulled out a similar Lightsaber with a retractable blade, only thicker, and pushed a button on the side- it hummed to life illuminating the boys in a green glow. "I have two."

Todd's eyes went wide. "Amazing!"

"And there's more."

"More?"

"Much more!" Charlie pulled out yet another Lightsaber-a blue one. "I figured you'd want a Saber of your own. We could have a battle. What do you say?"

"I say lets go."

They could have battled in Todd's yard, but there wouldn't be any obstacles to perform leaps and stunts off of. So, in a quick decision, they decided on Fountain City Park with plenty of space- slides, jungle gyms, swings, picnic tables, and a creek. It was heaven to a child.

Charlie extended his Saber, brought it to life and twirled it in his hands and said, "You ready for this?"

Todd ignited his own Saber, balanced himself in battle formation and replied, "It's on."

And they were off. Blade against blade, they imitated an actual Lightsaber battle. Each boy was in their own imaginative world. They jumped across the creek and Charlie ran up a slide where he then jumped off the opposite end. In midair, he swung his blade and was blocked by Todd's. He landed on his feet and the battle was still in full force.

It was Todd's turn to make a tricky move. He stepped up on a table and planned to jump off. In mid jump, he miscalculated the twist and Charlie sliced him in the stomach. Todd groaned and grabbed a hold of his stomach as he tumbled to the ground where he dropped the Saber by his side. Pretending to take his last breath, he said, "Well played."

Todd closed his eyes to imitate death, only the darkness grew darker as a shadow hovered over him. He kept his eyes closed as someone picked up his Saber and said to Charlie, "You have won this battle, but the war still fights on."

'Hannah?' Todd thought to himself. He opened his eyes to see Hannah lunge at Charlie with his Saber in hand. They were in an even more intense battle- this girl had skills.

Charlie grinned from ear to ear, even though, unbeknownst to him that he had met his match. She guided his steps backward where he had nowhere to see and concentrated only on the swings of her blade. He tripped over a tree root and landed flat on his back; he looked up at her astonished.

Hannah stepped over him and planted her blade to his neck and said, "Master Charlie, you have met your maker. Bow down to me, or taste sweet death."

Before Charlie could choose his destiny, laughter burst out from a group of adults on a picnic table nearby.

"Wow, you all are still a bunch of nerds." Ricky had stated.

"Oh no," Charlie muttered under his breath. The color faded from his face.

"Do you know these hoodlums?" Hannah asked.

"Welllll, lookie here, lookie here." Jill walked up to Charlie and said, "It's Brad's little brother."

"Oh snap, I didn't even recognize him." Derek added.

"Leave him alone, Jill. You know if Brad knew we were messing with him, he'd kill us." Logan insisted.

"Oh please, we're doing him a favor and ending what we started years ago." Jill turned to Charlie and with an evil grin flicked him on the nose.

Hannah stepped in and said, "Why don't you just leave him alone like the man said."

"Girrrl, you don't know who you're messing with. You best be getting goin." Jill replied.

Todd walked up, he knew what Charlie's anger could do. He saw the same look in Charlie's eyes and knew that if things did escalate, they wouldn't be pretty.

It didn't help that Derek chimed in and said, "Ooh, little Charlie has a girl doing his fighting for him. Do you see this?"

"Yeah, yeah I see it! Get 'em Jill, whoo hoo!" Stan cheered it on.

Jill just rolled her eyes.

"No, *you* don't know who *you* are messing with." Hannah held the saber out. "If you think we are nerdy and want someone to fight then I challenge you to a duel. Though, if you don't accept, then you can just leave us be."

"Okay, that's it-" Jill reached around and grabbed Hannah's hair, but just as quick as she grabbed it, she let go. Hannah smashed the rear end of the Saber on Jill's nose.

Blood poured out as Jill screamed, "You little devil, you broke my nose!"

"Umm de ja vu?" Derek asked.

"I told you not to mess with me, didn't I?" Hannah asked.

Jill turned to the gang, "What are you all sitting around for? Get her!"

They all sat, confused on what to do. Ricky spoke up, "Um Jill, I don't think we are supposed to hit a girl."

"And you better not either." An unfamiliar voice said. No one noticed Jim standing alone with a cup holder of three hot beverages from Pedal Java. "If I find out ANY of you laid a finger on this little girl, then you have *me* to answer to."

"Dad!" Todd was just as surprised to see his father.

Stan asked, "That's your dad?!" In a flash, he, Ricky, and Derek were gone. They ran off faster than their feet could take them-literally, because Stan tripped over the same root Charlie did and then kept on running.

"Sorry about this, sir." Logan lowered his head as he walked passed Jim.

Jill pointed back and forth between the three kids and said, "This isn't over! Either one of you!"

"Oh I believe it is." Hannah never left eye contact.

Jill squeezed a fist, but huffed and walked away when Logan yelled out, "Jill! Lets go!"

"Are you okay?" Jim turned to ask Charlie. "They didn't touch any of you did they?"

"I'm okay, Da- Jim." Charlie pushed the blade back inside the handle of his Saber.

"They only pulled Hannah's hair, but she took care of it." Todd informed him.

"Good girl." Jim smiled. "Here's a hot chocolate for everyone. I knew there had to be a reason I bought an extra one. Now I know why."

"Thanks!" They all said.

"Hannah, right?" Jim asked. He turned to Todd, "Isn't that the girl you have been swooning over?"

"Oh geez, thanks dad." Todd turned his head to hide the blush.

"Aww, he has?" Hannah smiled. "That's cute."

"Of course he has," Jim continued, "I couldn't tell you how much he's talked about you. I think he likes you."

Todd didn't want to look at Hannah and see her reaction. If he wasn't embarrassed before, he sure was now.

"That's okay with me, Mr. Clinton." Hannah said. "Could you tell Todd that I like him too?"

"You bet. Now, what's this Mr. Clinton, stuff? You can call me Jim." Jim stated.

"*Score*." Todd thought to himself. He wasn't sure if she liked him like he wished, or if they were just messing with him-which was a common thing in the Clinton household. Although, it didn't help that when Hannah told everyone bye later that day, she kissed Todd on the cheek before riding off on her bike.

Chapter Thirteen

(2001)

"Charlie, are you okay?" Jim asked as they left the park and drove down the road.

As Charlie stared out the window he said, "Yeah, I guess."

"That was awesome what Hannah did, huh?" Todd turned around to ask.

"Yeah, it was." Charlie said.

"Well, how come you didn't help out, Todd?" Jim asked. "When I got there, you were just standing there."

"I don't know." Todd suddenly felt ashamed.

"Look, it's okay to fight, but only fight for the right reasons. Like today, if you were to have jumped in and protected your friends then that's okay. Now, what they did by starting a fight for no good reason is wrong. And definitely, never, ever hit a woman. You wouldn't be a man if you lay your hands on a woman." Jim continued.

"I completely understand."

"Hey," Charlie spoke up, "can we please not talk about fighting for a while? I'm just so sick of fighting."

"Yeah, sure little buddy. No worries." Jim responded.

They drove in silence for a moment until Todd asked Jim, "Hey, do you still have your old tent? Could you take Charlie and me camping tonight?"

"Good idea!" Jim asked Charlie, "Is that okay with you?"

The dread look on Charlie's face was quickly replaced with a smile, "Sure!"

Later that night, they all laid under the stars on a clear cloudless night. There were no sounds except for the peaceful creatures of the night, the crackling of the fire, and the hum of Charlie's Lightsaber. Todd broke the silence and said, "Hey Charlie?"

"Hmm?" Charlie said.

"What are you thinking about?"

"Honestly? I'm thinking about my brother. I wonder how he's doing. I don't get to see him much- my foster parents won't let me."

"It's your family though...I mean, blood family."

"I know, they just say it's for my best."

"Parents are funny like that, and they are right, so at least they know what they are doing."

"I guess." Charlie sighed. He was silent for a moment before he said, "She likes you, you know?"

This caught Todd by surprise, "Who?"

"Hannah. And, I know you like her too."

"Oh man, very much. How can you tell?"

"You light up when she's around. I couldn't tell you how big your grin gets when you see her. And also, with her, she's so happy when you are near her. I don't know, it's just obvious."

"Oh, well cool. What should I do?"

"Dude," Charlie said, "There's no question about it, get her before it's too late- before she slips through your fingers."

"But, what if you liked her too? I mean, if I did go for her, I wouldn't want this to turn into a triangle love affair where both friends love the same girl and it causes trouble between them."

"Oh no, don't worry about that. I like her, don't get me wrong, but not in that way. Not like you do. You, my friend, deserve her. And let me tell you this, any girl to jump in and have a laser battle with you is a keeper."

"Ha, yeah that was awesome! And you know what was funny about that? She beat *you*."

"Hey, I tripped, okay...the sun was in my eyes."

Both boys burst out in laughter. Todd said, "Ohh, that girl's amazing."

"Welll, what do you plan on doing about it?" Charlie asked.

"I really don't know. Do you have any ideas?"

"Hmm..." Charlie thought to himself. "I've got it! There's a dance next Friday night, why don't you start out by asking her to that? And then at the dance, make her yours."

"That could work."

"It's got to. The ladies love dancing. Eat your heart out, Sinatra, Todd Clinton's on the town."

Chapter Fourteen

(2001)

Monday morning came around, the weekend passed by in a flash. Todd anxiously waited outside of English class for Hannah. He couldn't stand still and looked up when Charlie walked up to him and said, "Dude, calm down. You know she's going to say yes."

"Yeah, but it's the point of asking the initial question."

"Write her a note."

"Oh please, I'm not that nerdy..." Todd looked down the other end of the hallway and continued, "Okay, maybe I am, but notes are so cheesy."

"Not to the guys who wrote love letters all the time-especially if you are trying to serenade her with romance. Girls love cheesy romance."

"That makes me wonder how your brother got his girlfriend."

"Oh, that's a different situation- they're both crazy, and two crazies make a whole."

"You think?" Todd asked.

"Hey, I know so." Charlie said as he noticed Hannah walking their way. "Okay, Todd, breathe and act natural."

"Hey guys!" Hannah smiled as she walked up to the boys. "How was your all's weekend? Well, despite your utter battle cry, Charlie."

"Hey, I tripped! Or rather, that root attacked me. It was an unfair advantage." Charlie said.

"I thought you told me the sun was in your eyes?" Todd chimed in.

"I don't have to take this abuse, I'm going to class." Charlie stepped inside, but stuck his head out the door and whispered to Todd and winked, "Ask her."

"Ask me what?" Hannah asked, but she suspected what was coming.

"Oh uh, how was your weekend?" Todd spirted out.

The bell to warn there was 5 minutes before class started ringing out in the hall. As Hannah and Todd entered in the classroom she said, "It was well. Oh, your parents said to thank your dad for the hot chocolate and saving us from those goons."

"It was nothing, that's dad for you. He has a heart of a hero."

"Well I hope his son does too." Hannah sat in her seat and was getting all her books and papers ready for class.

Charlie leaned over and kicked Todd who still stood by his desk. When Todd looked down at him, he mouthed, "Ask her!"

Todd took a deep breath, sat down at his desk and said, "Hey Hannah?"

"Sup?" she turned around.

"Do you have any plans Friday?"

"Umm, no- not that I know of."

"Would you likekekdidngo?" Todd slurred.

"I'm sorry, what?" Hannah asked and burst into laughter. Todd's face went red.

Charlie's eyes went wide and couldn't believe what he had just seen. "I believe he said, 'Would you like to go the dance with me?'"

Todd gave Charlie the thumbs up and said, "What he said."

"Yes, I'd love to go to the dance with you, Todd." Hannah smiled, patted Todd's arm and then turned back around as the teacher started the lesson.

Charlie whispered to Todd, "What would you do without me?"

***

The following Friday, both Todd and Charlie got ready in Todd's room after school. It had been each of theirs first dances and Todd, for sure, didn't know what to do. Butterflies had a hold of his stomach and he couldn't kick any of the nervous feelings inside.

"How come you didn't ask anyone to go with you?" Todd asked Charlie as he combed his hair.

"I just don't want to date some random person. When it's the right time and the right person, God will make it happen."

"Wow, that was deep."

"You know what I've been through, though; I've seen what happens when God is not in the picture, but yet, He is always there- so I keep a positive attitude that He will pull through."

They had arrived at the dance a little too early and helped the DJ set up his equipment in the cafeteria- where the tables and chairs were moved to one side of the room and streamers were hung from the ceiling. It wasn't long after that, that the kids arrived- some were dressed nice, and others came as they were. The main lights were shut off, and multicolored spot lights were tuned on, along with a disco ball in the middle of the room.

"Do you see the irony in this?" Charlie laughed as they sat at a table waiting for Hannah.

"What's that?" Todd asked.

"During school, we sit in the back of the room away from everyone, and yet, even though it's after hours and we are technically in school- we are still sitting alone."

Todd laughed. "That is ironic; maybe 'cause we are nerds and that makes us even more awesome than everyone else."

Charlie glanced at a group of teens who were practically dancing up against each other and said, "Umm, yeah, you are definitely right about that." He pointed to the group, "And *that* is the very reason we are awesome. We are nothing like them- the 'popular' crowd."

"Hey, it was your idea to come to this shindig."

"We're not here for *them*, we're here for Hannah. It's your 'Carpe Diem' moment."

"My what?"

"It's your moment to seize the day- make it yours. I know it's going to happen. And Todd, I need you to turn around and take a look at who just walked in."

Todd got excited and quickly turned around in his chair. "Who am I looking at?"

"No one, I'm messing with you." Charlie chuckled.

"That's not funny." Todd stated.

"Sure it is, you're tense. Loosen up; if you're going to dance with her tonight, you don't want to be stiff like that."

"Oh...crap. I didn't think about that. I'm in trouble, I don't know how to dance."

"Why don't you ask Principal Gennings to teach you how real fast? Or even the janitor. I'm sure they would *love* to teach you. Not me though, I'm only here for the show."

"No thank you, there's only one person I'd rather dance with tonight."

"And I hope that person is me." Hannah said as she snuck up behind Todd.

Todd looked up and immediately locked his eyes on hers. She was dressed in a thin long baby blue dress, hair curled, and had on blue converse shoes. "You look amazing." Todd said.

"Aww, thank you. That's sweet of you." Hannah blushed. She was glad to finally see Todd coming out of his shell.

He scooted over and asked, "Would you like to sit down?"

"Why yes I would." Hannah said and sat down next to Todd. She looked across the table at Charlie who had a cheesy grin on his face. "What is it?"

"I'm just shocked." Charlie then said to Todd, "I don't mean to embarrass you, but I've got to say it, I'm really shocked with Todd. When we were kids he saved me from bullies, but with you he's really shy. I just think it's funny."

"Did he now?" Hannah smiled and then looked at Todd, "I knew he had a hero's heart as well."

It was Todd's turn to blush, but he said to Hannah, "I could be your hero."

"I would like that a lot." Hannah put her hand in his. He was sure his hands were sweaty, but she didn't seem to care and still held on.

The first slow song of the night started, and Todd knew it was now or never to make a fool of himself, he asked, "Would you like to dance?"

"Yes I would," Charlie cut in.

"Not you, her." Todd stated.

"Well fine then, be that way." Charlie smiled.

Todd led Hannah to the dance floor and they danced in perfect time. He must have been a natural- with a twirl, he placed his hand on the small of her back and held her hand with the other. In sync with the music, they didn't speak for the next couple of minutes and were completely lost in each other's eyes.

All at the same time, Charlie watched one of the few people in this world that meant everything to him fall for another person of that select few as well. He was happy for them and happy where God placed him in his life. Because of his past, Charlie learned to live in the moment, and the moment was grand.

Then when the song was over, they made their way back to the table still hand in hand. Charlie said to Todd, "See, I told you, you could dance. And you didn't need the Principal to help you."

"Thank heavens for that." He replied. "Otherwise I'd be dancing alone air guitar style."

"Hey, I'm down with that. I call an air guitar dance off." Hannah said.

The look on Charlie's face was priceless and said, "Brilliant idea! Todd, you know you've found a keeper right?"

"And what makes me a keeper?" Hannah asked.

"You're a nerd, just like us." Charlie said. "Nerds need to stick together. And of course, you and Todd will make the cutest couple."

"I most certainly am a nerd, I can't lie about that. And I'm sure he and I would if that's something he would want. I do admit, I love that you are implying it though." Hannah said.

"Oh there's no *would* about that, I *do* want to be with you. God wouldn't have had us meet if He didn't have a reason." Todd implied.

"Amen to that!" Hannah said, "I know right now though, not to bust anyone's spirits, but my dad says I'm too young to date. I do think God had us all meet for a reason, even though we don't know what reason that is, but He still brought forth a nerdy friendship."

"Preach it sister!" Charlie yelled.

The rest of the evening was spent in laughter and good times. They danced, they played, they were caught in the moment of fellowship with one another. Todd didn't get around to asking Hannah to be his since she said she was too young, but he knew his time was just around the corner.

Chapter Fifteen

(2001)

Today was Brad's birthday, which out in the real world he'd be celebrating with his friends as they bar hopped from one bar to the next- but instead, the only bar, Brad, was able to hop on, on his 21st birthday was the bars of his jail cell.

Brad was alone and completely miserable. Since he had been in there, he had not heard a single word from his mom, his brother, nor even his "friends"- the same friends who were supposed to be there for him no matter what. And yet, because he was miserable, all he could do was lay there and let his anger of the world subside in him, laying on his stomach like bricks. This day, of all days, couldn't get any worse.

However as he laid there he didn't expect to hear from a guard, "Dunn! You have a visitor!"

'Oh no, not you,' Brad thought to himself as he saw who the visitor was. He sighed as he picked up the phone and asked, "What in the world are you doing here?"

"How are you doing, Brad? Happy birthday." Bill said with a calm to his voice.

"Wow...really? Tell it to somebody who cares." Brad went to hang up the phone.

"Brad wait! Please! Can you just give me one minute? Please, son."

Brad held the phone down at his waist and screamed out harsh obscenities and sat back down because of the guard's strict gaze. He said, "Fine...go."

"I just wanted to tell you, that I'm truly sorry. For everything. I have not been a good dad to you, or a dad at all. But, I'm sorry and hope you will forgive me."

The look of pure anger that came across Brad's face made Bill uncomfortable. He was silent, but Bill still pleaded, "Brad, please say something."

"Listen here, and you better listen to me good. Because of you, I'm in this place for who knows how long.

Because of you, I have to spend my 21ˢᵗ birthday with no party whatsoever. Because of you, I've lost everything, including any ounce of happiness that was in my life. Not a chance will I ever forgive you. And you have some nerve to come down here and ask me that. Well, guess what, you've wasted your time."

He hung up the phone and headed back to his cell. Not once, did he turn around to see if his father was still sitting there, nor did he even care if he made him cry.

Chapter Sixteen

(2001)

It took everything in Brad's power to control his anger until he got back to his cell. If anyone was to cross his path the wrong way, it wouldn't have been a pretty outcome. And there was no telling if that person would still be living or not if Brad was to take out his frustrations on them.

As luck may have it, all his anger subsided when he made it back to his cell and saw that he had a new cell mate, and said, "Yes! I can't believe it. Finally, some support in this place. I was in certain need of some good cheer. How've you been, Logan?"

"Not bad, not bad. Talk about a small world, huh? Who would've thought we'd be cell mates?"

"Makes perfect sense to me; bros have got to stick together. We've made it through and through and here we are again. Life is looking good after all." Brad said.

"*This* is a good life?" Logan stretched out his arms to show he meant the cell.

"Trust me, it's not so bad once you get the hang of it." Brad flopped down on his bed. "The food is terrible though, and it's freezing a lot. But, it's better than the streets, that's for sure."

"I don't know if I can get used to this..."

"One way or the other, you're going to have to. Nothing else to it. Might as well just relax and take it easy, no need to walk treads in the floor."

Logan finally did sit down on the bed, but yet, still tense.

"So, you know this question was coming- what you in for?" Brad asked.

"Drinking and driving and ended up killing someone."

"Crap...what happened?"

"We had left a party and the guy with me was so messed up more than usual. He kept poking at me and grabbing the wheel and so I lost it- I yelled at him and lost control of the car. We then crashed head on into a fast food restaurant. Derek flew out of the windshield and was smashed in between the car and building. I was out cold and couldn't tell anyone he was there. They just assumed the blood was ketchup."

"Wow, Der-" Brad teared up. "I just knew something bad would happen to him. He was just a crazy little punk."

"Yeah...right."

"How's everyone else, though? Everybody still kicking it?"

"Basically. I haven't been around much since Jill and Ricky pretty much have become more ruthless than before. And, of course, Derek and Stan had to tag along in all their shenanigans." Logan said.

"Why does that not surprise me with those goons? I can't say much, you guys were all I had. Without you all, I had nothing. I can't wait to get out of here, get with Jill, and then get back to the way things were. Which, speaking of, why did none of you all keep in touch?"

"Yeah...umm, that's not going to happen. The night you were taken in, Jill and Ricky hooked up and have been together ever since."

"What?! That traitor! I knew she was sleeping with him behind my back. I just KNEW it! Man, why did you let me sit here and praise those back stabbing-" Brad stopped himself and sat up. "Never mind, it's not worth it. I've got something else to take care of."

Chapter Seventeen

(2001)

Brad was furious once again, but he held it in. The guards let him make a phone call, and there was only one person he wanted to talk to. Hopefully this time, out of many calls over the years, he could get through to her...

"MMM, ello?" Jill's words slurred. Loud music blared along with a crowd in the background. "Hehe, stop I Ricky, I'm on the phone."

"A little drunk aren't we?" Brad kept his cool.

"Well, maybe a whittle."

"That's what I thought."

"Why don't you come join us?"

"Yeahhh, I kind of can't right now. I'm in prison."

"Ha-ha, that stinks. Who is this?"

"It's Brad."

"Brad...Brad! Hi! Oh, Brad, I've missed you!"

"Brad?" Ricky asked from the background. He yelled over Jill's shoulder, "Hey! How you been doing, buddy?"

"You've missed me, huh? Why haven't none of you kept in touch?" Brad asked.

"We have, you never answer your phone." Jill said.

"That's because I'm in prison!"

"Oh...oopsie, he-he."

"Oopsie is right. Oh well, I don't have much time, so I just called to let you know I've always known about you and Ricky- so, have a good life together you two-timing, low-life, back stabbing jerks. And, you better be lucky I'm not there, because both of you would be a little swollen in the morning. You best believe that."

I'm done with you all and this so-called 'gang'. Forget you all." Brad slammed down the phone. He felt surprisingly good with cutting off most of his ties. Now it was just Logan and himself- his best friend was all he needed.

Chapter Eighteen

(2001)

Jill threw her phone across the room and yelled, "The nerve of that guy, I swear!"

"What baby? What happened?" Ricky held on to her as he kissed her shoulder.

"Brad! He really doesn't know who he's messing with- calls up and throws us to the wind. Look at all we've done for that jerk and look at how he treats us."

"I know! He's a jerk."

"Major jerk!"

"We need to get back at him."

"Word! We do!" Jill said, "We need to teach him a lesson so good he'll never forget."

"Never!" Ricky yelled.

"No never! I swear, I'll get my revenge one day. You just watch."

"No never! I swear, I'll get my revenge one day. You just watch."

Chapter Nineteen

(2004)

Three years have passed. Charlie, Todd, and Hannah remained the best of friends. Together, they made it through Junior High, and started over at the bottom of the barrel with their freshman year in high school, but they made it through that. Nerdy as ever, they stuck together and kept to themselves- despite traditional high school cliques. They were just themselves.

Now, as sophomores, Charlie was the first of their clan to get his driver's license. He passed the test with flying colors- though in his mind, he drove through the road proportion of the test as if he was casually flying the Millennium Falcon. And that, the Force guided him along the way. It worked though, so no complaints there.

He knew that with his foster parents paying for his insurance on his Pinto, it was his job to pay for the gas. So, he needed a job. Where he lived, nothing interested him enough to work, and on top of that, they all required experience and a college degree before hire. Part time was the only option for him due to his school schedule, and so dressed in a suit and tie, he sat in the local coffee shop as he read the job ads. It, of course, made him look much older than he really was, but the owner of the shop had taken a notice of Charlie.

The owner was shorthanded, but Charlie could be the employee he was looking for as well. He said, "Excuse me, son."

Charlie looked around before he realized the gentleman behind the counter was talking to him. "Me?"

"Yes, you. Come here for a second. What's your name?"

"Charlie Dunn."

"Hi, Charlie, my name's Max Helton. Have you worked in a coffee shop before?"

"No, I've just drank a lot of it, especially from Pedal Java. I LOVE that place. I haven't worked anywhere yet, to be honest. I'm looking for work though."

"How old are you?"

"Just turned 16."

"How would you feel like working for me? I need the help."

"Great! Yes, I'd love to work here. When could I start?"

It was a Saturday morning, and Max knew he had school on Monday, so he offered, "How does Monday around 5 sound?"

"That sounds great to me!"

"Okay, good deal. All I need is for you to fill out some paperwork and we'll be good to go."

"Just like that?"

"Just like that." Max smiled.

Charlie walked out after he finished his coffee both excited and extremely happy. He looked up to the sky and said, "Thank you, Lord."

***

Monday afternoon, Charlie walked into the coffee shop with a skip to his walk. He had a new haircut, new khaki pants and a polo shirt- he was ready to work.

Max introduced him to his coworkers and took the day training and showing him the ropes. Charlie caught on quick- so quick that by then end of the night he was practically running the place. All of the employees, even Max, were completely shocked at how passionate Charlie was at becoming a barista. No, not 'becoming', he was a natural.

At the end of the day, everyone dragged their feet and were ready to go home, but Charlie was pumped and wanted to keep on going. He knew though, that tomorrow was a new day. He had found his calling in life, and he didn't know just how much of a calling being a barista would be in his life. All the thanks he could give were to God, as well as Andy and Ashley (Andy's wife) at Pedal Java who gave him the inspiration.

Chapter Twenty

(2004)

Charlie, Hannah, and Todd sat outside at the bench tables for lunch. Todd said to Charlie, "Hey man, you working this weekend? Or Friday night?"

"Oh yes!" Charlie smiled.

"Well...what?" Todd asked again.

Hannah said, "Charlie, I love you, but you're the first person I've known to be excited over work. You give me hope that there's still crazy left in this world."

"Hey, I love my job, I'm like the caffeine bartender." Charlie replied. "People come to me with their problem of exhaustion, and I give the solution. And they give me smiles, so it's a win/win situation."

"Okay, so what are you going to do if..." Todd began, "if an angry, lunatic, business man comes in and demands his coffee because he's more rich and better than you coffee servants?"

"Easy, I 'accidentally' give him a cup of decaf, smile, and send him on his way." Charlie said.

"Like your manager would be okay with you doing that." Todd said.

"Oh no, he's all up for it after an angry customer threw their cup of coffee back at him when it didn't taste the way he wanted it to."

"Hmm, interesting." Todd placed a piece of cord on his spoon and launched it across the lunch area and said, "Awesome."

"I think that's really great, Charlie, that you are so happy, especially after what all you told me about your childhood." Hannah encouraged.

"Hey, it's cool. I'm me, and that's all that matters." Charlie finished his can of soda and threw it behind him. He hoped to make it in the trash can without looking, but it was a total miss. He said, "Man, be right back."

Todd launched another piece of corn. It hit Charlie in the back of the head. "Punk!"

"Score!" Todd menacingly laughed. He turned to Hannah who sat beside him and said, "Sooo, what about you? What are you doing Friday night?"

She shrugged her shoulders. "I dunno, I never really do anything except read. Typical Friday for me."

"Yeah, me either." Todd was quiet for a moment, until a light bulb went off and he said, "Hey, here's a thought, IF your folks allow it, what do you say we go on a date?"

She had wanted to date Todd for years, but knew her parents would have never allowed it. They were in high school now, and things could be different. She said, "I'm going to say yes, but we'll see after what they say."

"Well, they love me, so it should be okay. And you just smiling over there makes me happy, even if they do say no."

"You're real sweet, do you know that? And yes, they do love you, like I love you."

***

It was Hannah's turn to do the dishes. She was quiet as she scrubbed the dishes, deep in thought about how she was going to ask her parents about Todd. This was something she has waited for since she met Todd, but now that she had the chance, she didn't want to mess it up.

As she rinsed the dishes, her mother stepped up beside her and said, "Hunny, are you okay? You've been quiet tonight."

"Oh yeah, mom. I'm fine. I just got a lot on my mind at the moment."

"You aren't pregnant are you?" Her father asked while he worked on a jigsaw puzzle from the dining room table.

"Dad!"

"What? I'm just asking."

"No, I'm not pregnant. I've never even gone on a date." Here goes nothing. "But that's kind of what is on my mind right now."

"Hannah," her father said, "stop right there, you've already had the talk. There's no reason to be thinking of pregnancy."

"What? No, I wasn't thinking of that. I was thinking how you all would feel if I went on a date tomorrow night. Would that be okay?"

"Well, yeah. You've been dating Todd for a while now." Her mother said.

"No I haven't, you always told me I was too little. I wanted to for a long time though." Hannah stated.

"Oh no, that was just your dad being silly. No boy would ever be good enough for him. But, Todd, is different. We've always liked him. If you would have said so when you met him, we would've been okay with it."

"Gee, thanks. I wish I had known that sooner. I love that boy."

***

Charlie's shift had started, but yet the evening wasn't as busy as usual. He and the other employees stood around mostly and joked around. In walked Hannah and Todd. Charlie said, "Hey guys! Geez, even on a first date you couldn't get away from me."

"Oh you know, we had nothing better to do." Todd laughed. "We were going to go to a movie, but there wasn't anything good playing."

"I couldn't tell you the last movie I saw." Charlie said, "Well, what could I get you guys?"

"Two coffees would be fine."

"Two coffees coming right up."

After they received their coffees, Todd and Hannah took a seat at the leather love seat in the corner. "This is really nice," Hannah said.

"Yeah it is, I'm still stoked your folks let you go-out with me."

"Why is that?"

"Look at you, I've loved you since the moment I first laid eyes on you." Todd said.

"But you didn't know me yet, how did you know you loved me?" Hannah asked. "I will admit though, I felt the same with you. When I saw you, that's where I felt drawn to, as if God was putting me in that exact spot at the right time. I remember the seat in front of you was empty and I just knew that seat was the seat for me."

"I can't explain how I knew, I just knew it. I think God was poking me and telling me, 'That's her.'"

"Oh, you think I'm the *one*, huh?"

"I would hope so. I mean, look at us, we're perfect for each other. Who goes on a first date in jeans and super hero t-shirts? And who loves Star Wars as much as we do?

On top of that, we love God and church." Todd said. "It's meant to be- at least that's what I believe. I don't want just one date with you, I want many more with you."

"I completely agree with you. I never wanted to be the type of girl to go from one guy to the next. If I want to be with someone, I want it to last and be forever. And with you, Todd Clinton, I believe as well it's meant to be. You are one special guy."

"Took you this long to figure that out?"

"Nope, I've always known it. You just didn't show how special you were because of your shyness."

"I wasn't that shy." Todd stated.

"Oh, please."

"Okay...maybe just a little bit."

"Maybe just a lot." Hannah laughed.

Todd sipped on his coffee and said, "Hannah, I don't want this night to end. I know that was totally random, but I want you to know that. I've always loved you. Will you be my girlfriend?"

"See, that's the Todd I love, you're a romantic and you show it. Of course I'll be your girlfriend. I wouldn't have it any other way."

Charlie watched the whole conversation from the counter and smiled. He knew there was something magical in a coffee atmosphere, and one day he'll share that magic with others.

Chapter Twenty-One

(2006)

As fast as high school began, it was over in a flash. Just days away from graduation.

Charlie clocked in to work, put on his apron and walked over to his cash register, when Max spoke from his office, "Hey Dunn, come here for a minute. I need to talk to you."

"What's up, Max?"

"Sit down, you should hear this." Max sat at the edge of his desk. "What are you planning for your life after you graduate?"

"To be honest, *this*. There's nowhere else I want to be. This place is my life. To most people, this isn't much, but to me, it's everything. I don't need a lot."

"That's what I thought. You've been loyal to this job since day one. I see the spark in your eye that I had when I started the company years ago. That's why I'm offering you the management position, pay raise, and benefits. What do you say?"

Charlie almost fell out of his seat. "I say, sign me up. This is my home."

Max held out his hand. "Okay then, lets make it official, Mr. Dunn."

***

That night when Charlie walked out of work, he felt almost complete. Through all of God's trials and tribulations in his short lived life, *this* was a blessing to him. He knew his family would be proud of him, and knew that was part of why he didn't feel complete. He forgave his mother and his father and gave that up to God, because that was all he could do. With his brother though, it was much harder. His parents didn't hurt him like his brother did. He knew where Brad was all this time, but never went to see him. Charlie knew, this was the best time to make that happen and make things right before it was too late.

When Brad got the news that he had a visitor-which he never did-he swore up and down that if it was Bill, he'd have nothing to do with him and refuse the visit. Though, when he saw that it was Charlie sitting there in his work uniform it took him by surprise. He was all grown up and it took the breath right out of him. He didn't know what to feel- except any anger he had for the world, for that moment, was completely gone. Only thing though, he felt grief, for at that moment he realized how much he had missed out in Charlie's life.

As he sat down, his hands shook as he picked up the phone. It took all he could not to let out the tears in his eyes. He was taught to always be tough and never cry in prison, it showed weakness. He sobbed, "Charlie?"

"In the flesh."

"Man, I never thought I'd ever see you again. How are you?"

"Excellent! You look different...clean, actually." Charlie said.

"Hey, not being on drugs or drunk for twelve years would do a number on you." For the first time in a long time Brad actually laughed. It was different, for sure.

"I bet." Charlie suddenly realized he didn't know what to say. He was glad to see Brad, but a part of him wouldn't let go of the night he last saw him. He said a silent prayer to himself, *'Lord, help me.'*

"It's good to see you, Charlie. If it was anyone else, like Bill, I would've jumped through this glass and killed him."

"I guess things haven't changed as much as I thought they would. Sorry I wasted your time." Charlie started to put the phone back in its cradle.

"No, no, wait, wait." Brad stopped him. "You haven't wasted my time, honestly. What makes you think you have?"

"I don't know, you still seem to have all that anger and resentment. I loved you, but I resented you at the same time. It scared me every time you were around. I even called you Lord Zedd and Jill was Rita." Charlie chuckled. "You know, from Power Rangers? Anyway, but, with dad I've never seen him since he left, but I forgive him. And mom as well, even though she's completely whacko. That wasn't her fault though."

"Charlie..." Brad could see something coming over Charlie, something pushing to come out.

"Hang on, let me finish." Charlie said, "I came here to forgive you, to tell you I didn't deserve the way you and your friends treated me. Why couldn't you have just loved me? I lost dad, mom, and you. But I'm okay, I made it. I'm graduating in a few days, and I've been promoted to manager at a coffee shop. I'm happy, but I can't keep living without forgiving you, but it's so hard right now. All I can see is that last night I saw you."

"Charlie, I'm so sorry, okay? I really am. I was young, stupid, and yes, I didn't know any better. You're right- you didn't deserve that." Brad wiped the tears from his eyes and for the first time felt ashamed and guilty for his actions. "I don't expect you to forgive me, I can't tell you how sorry I am."

This was Charlie's chance, he knew what had to be done. He forgave Brad right then and there in his heart and smiled, "Okay, so, lets start back from when we last spoke…I'm sorry as well for beating the snot out of you with my Lightsaber."

Brad burst out in laughter that took even the guards by surprise. Up until that time he was a hard inmate to deal with and hardly ever smiled. A part of them believed he too lost it and went crazy on them.

"Wow…sorry, I needed that laugh." Brad said, catching his breath. "No, don't be sorry, I deserved that. I forgive you, but we're brothers, we fight. And to be honest, I forgot all about it until now, which it's actually quite comical. Think about it, I got beat up by a kindergartner with a toy Lightsaber- how pathetic am I?"

"So, you aren't mad at me? And yeah…you got knocked out, son!" The inmate down from Brad gave Charlie an evil look after he imitated his gangsta voice. Charlie mouthed the word, "Sorry."

"No, no, I'm not mad at you. Shew…" Brad thought for a moment. "Is that why mom went whacko?"

"Yeah…she had a mental break down and hasn't recovered since. Because of it, I was sent to a foster home. I can't complain though, I mean, they've been really good to me."

The color from Brad's face faded. "Charlie…I'm so sorry. I didn't know. I- Why did I have to be so stupid?"

"Brad, listen man, it's really okay. God had a bigger plan for you, for all of us. It's hard to see, but He isn't done with us yet. You've just got to see the beauty from the clouds."

"I've never been a believer, so I don't know what to think of that. That sent my mind in a whirlwind."

"Just leave it up to God. That's all we can do, and pray."

"I don't know if I can do that."

"How about this, I'll lend you my bible, and when you are ready you can read it all you want. Okay?"

"Okay…yeah." Brad wasn't sure what was going on inside of him.

"Times up Dunn!" a guard yelled.

"Guess I got to go. It's been good seeing you, Brad." Charlie said.

"You take care little brother, come see me again." Brad turned to walk away, but picked up the phone again and said, "I'm really proud of you Charlie, you're a fine young man."

Chapter Twenty-Two

(2006)

Todd sat in his car with the pouring rain pounding on his windshield. He held the final letter from the last college applied for and contemplated on if he should open it or not. Talk about the last minute. He could just hear Hannah's voice inside his head, *"Well, aren't you going to open it?"*

"Maybe."

"Why maybe?"

"Because this is the rest of my life in my hands. It determines our future." Todd said. He sighed and ripped open the seal, pulled out the letter and read: *Dear, Mr. Clinton, unfortunately-*

He crumpled up the letter and tossed it in the passenger floorboard. It wasn't supposed to be this way. He knew he had to tell Hannah, but he just didn't want to break her heart, not this close to graduation. Instead, he decided on giver her an amazing final date before she headed off to college, and he...he would still be back home.

***

Hannah couldn't decide on what dress she was going to wear to graduation. Dress after dress was scattered amongst her bed, along with the stuffed animals Todd had bought her over the years. A knock came from her door and she said, "Come in."

Todd entered in.

"Todd! Thank heavens you're here. Which dress do you think I should wear for graduation?"

"Aren't you supposed to wear a cap and gown?"

"Yes, but I have to wear a dress underneath, silly. So, what do you choose?" She asked.

He barely even glanced at the dresses and held his head down, "I don't know."

"Are you okay? You look sick."

Todd tried to hide away his gloom and acted happy, "Oh yea, sorry, I was lost in thought. Say, what are you doing tomorrow night? I just want to take you on a date."

"Well of course you can sweetie."

"Okay, good deal."

Later that evening as Todd left Hannah's house, he couldn't shake the hurt he felt inside. He hated going through the night acting as if nothing was bothering him. Let alone keeping it from Hannah. Either way, he just knew he'd break her heart. It was something he couldn't do.

At home, he made his way to his bedroom, dragging his feet along. As he listened to the pouring rain, he sat on the edge of his bed. On top of his desk, a box of memories of he and Hannah mocked him. He thought to himself, *'Don't do it, it'll only make things worse.'*

Against the pain, he moved to the desk and sat down and opened the box. They had so many memories between them from the past two years- even so that they filled up a photo album of pictures. Being with her was so right, he had to figure out *something*.

Chapter Twenty-Three

(2006)

Todd cancelled their date at the last minute. It was something he had never done, and something he knew he never wanted to do again.

He was white as a ghost when he walked in to the coffee shop. Charlie was the only one working at the moment and said, "Welcome to- oh man, Todd, are you okay?"

Todd sat down at the counter, shaking. "No buddy, I don't think I am."

"Here, on the house." Charlie handed him a cup of coffee. "What's wrong?"

"Man, I don't know what to do. I have such a dilemma, it's not even funny."

"Lets talk, you know I'm here to help."

"It's about Hannah and I." Todd said. "I didn't get into college, and she's going to New York. I don't have any money to go, there's nothing there for me."

"Have you talked to Hannah about it?"

"No I haven't...not yet at least. I'm scared to, because of the outcome."

"Look, man, I know you love her. You've wanted to be with this woman since we were still kids. Don't let something like this split you apart. There's got to be a way."

"Yeah, but *what* though? I've thought of everything possible. The two most logical explanations I can think of are me going with her or we go our separate ways."

"If I were you, I'd go with the first one. Go with her. Yeah you won't have anything, but at least you will be starting a whole new life with her. Talk it over with her, see what she says. It wouldn't hurt."

"Trust me, I want to."

"Then go, man. Graduation is tomorrow, you won't have much longer after that."

But of course, he didn't. Instead, he spent his evening laying in the dark at home trying to figure it all out.

***

The class of 2006 respectively stood, turned their tassels to the side and were officially graduates. Everyone cheered and screamed with joy as caps were thrown. Some kids cried and other ran knowing they were free. Todd, out of all, was the only kid not taking part of the festivities.

"Todd, Hunny, we did it! Be happy!" Hannah cheered. She hugged him and felt him stiff.

"I just can't, knowing this is all coming to an end."

"Oh, but it's not the end, though! Our lives have just begun!"

"That's not what I'm-" Todd was interrupted by Hannah's family pulling her away in hugs and congratulations.

"Sorry, Todd!" Hannah said. "I'll be right back."

"I take it you haven't talked to her?" Charlie asked behind Todd.

"No, I just couldn't." Todd replied.

"Don't put it off man, I'm telling you."

For some reason, Charlie's comment really hit Todd and not in a good way. All the pressure he had built up inside was far too much for Todd and he snapped, "Seriously, Charlie, really? Look man, happy graduation and all, but I don't need this right now. I can't be here."

And Todd ran, leaving Charlie stunned. He jumped in his car and drove on.

Of all places, Todd ended up at a liquor store. He had no clue what he was doing, but just wandered around the store. There were different kinds of drinks, but he decided on whiskey, because that's what all the broken hearted people drank in the movies. He had always heard it would help anyone who wanted to forget a pain. He didn't even think about being underage and just walked up to the counter like it was nothing and placed the bottle on top.

About that time, Jill, Ricky, and Stan walked in the door. Todd locked eyes with each of them as they passed. Time seemed to slow down, but when he turned back to the counter the bottle was gone. "Hey what-" Todd started to say.

"Son, don't even. I know you're not 21, so don't even try it." the clerk said.

"Oh come on, so what? Show some compassion, I just graduated. And I've got a lot on my mind. Can't you just let it slide this one little time?"

"No, I'm sorry, but I can't. Happy graduation though."

"Whatever." Todd stormed out.

He drove across the street to a gas station and bought himself a cup of coffee, not as good as Charlie's coffee, but it'll do. On the way back to his car, Jill and her friends pulled up next to him.

'*Great,*" Todd thought to himself.

Ricky stuck his head out of the window. "Todd, right?"

"Look, I'm not in the mood right now. If you are wanting to start something I'd advise you to just step off, unless you want your face knocked in."

"Whoa! Easy, Tiger." Jill said. "We don't know what's up, but we overheard you in the liquor store. We thought we'd help you out."

Ricky held out a brown paper bag with an obvious bottle of liquor inside.

"Umm, thanks?" Todd said.

"Have fun, and if you get caught, you didn't get that from us." Ricky rolled up the window and they drove off.

Todd went home and hid the bottle underneath his seat. He spent the evening with Jim as they had a cookout and talked about what was bothering Todd. And yet, even

Jim's advice would be for him to pray about it and talk it over with Hannah. God had to have a reason for it.

For the time being, he kept the bottle hid, and texted Hannah, "Hey, are you up?"

"Hey! Yes, I've been waiting on you to text me back. What's up?"

"Nothing, I'm just sitting here with dad. Can I see you? I need to talk to you about something."

"Yeah, sure."

Todd met up with her at the community park where they had their Lightsaber battle years ago. Hannah was concerned and said, "So what's been going on, Todd? This past week you've been distant from me and Charlie. Did we do something wrong? Did I?"

"Not at all, I promise. It's not you, but I can't lie...it does have to do about *us*." Todd reached in his pocket and pulled out a ball of paper and handed it to Hannah.

She opened it up and read the denied college application. "Oh, Todd. I'm so sorry. This was the last one, wasn't it?"

"Yeah...I just don't get why I wasn't accepted. I had the grades, but I'm guessing since I didn't have the money."

Hannah sobbed, "Now I see why this is about us…"

"I know, and it's killing me. I mean, what are we supposed to do?"

"I don't know." She turned her head so he couldn't see her cry.

"Hannah…"

"I don't get it, why didn't you tell me about this in the first place? Why bring this up, now?"

"Because I was scared of what it might mean. Scared of not being able to figure it out."

"I just want to be with you, Todd."

"And I want to be with you also."

She wiped the tears from her eyes. "Lets think rational about this. Why couldn't you just come to New York with me?"

"I thought of that, but you'll be staying in the dorms, where will I stay? I can't afford to live on my own. I don't have anywhere to go."

"Yeah, and if my dad found out we were staying together and not married he'd kill me."

"Which I don't want to put you in that position. Nor do I want you to stay here just for me. I know how much work you've done just to go to that school." Todd said.

"Now we're back to square one." Hannah said. They were silent for a moment, thinking. "Lets get married."

"What?"

"Do you want to get married?"

"If the circumstances were different I would in a heartbeat. I don't want to force you to get married. That would still leave us homeless. Believe me, I've thought about that." Todd bawled. "I can't take this! There's NOTHING we can do! I've wanted you for so long, and I don't want to give up now. I hate this! I really do!"

"It doesn't have to be over, Todd. We could make it work, people do have long distance relationships. We could text, talk every day, email, and see each other on breaks and holidays. We can make it work."

Todd just knew it wouldn't work that way, but he still agreed to keep Hannah assured. In the end, he just did it to avoid losing her completely. Until she went off to college, he wanted to spend every moment he could with her, in her arms.

Chapter Twenty-Four

(2006)

He had to admit his failure of not getting accepted to college, even as well that very change, changed every plan he made for the future. It hurt even worst as he watched Hannah pack up and drive off with him standing alone in her driveway. Todd never felt so alone. His dad had to work, and so did Charlie. There was nothing for him to do and it was then that he remembered the bottle of whisky under his driver's seat.

There was rumors of a party that evening for the graduates who celebrated their new freedom. Todd had never been to a party, but at the moment, one didn't sound half bad. He only wanted to clear his head.

When he arrived, it seemed like fun from the outside, but then on the inside, kids were drunk and dancing with each other- he didn't feel so comfortable after that. The house was by a lake, so he walked on through and by-passed the party altogether, and made his way down to the dock. There was a full moon out that night, so he sat on the edge, drank from his whiskey bottle and just watched the water. He didn't care how much of the time went by.

His phone rang, and even though he was still inebriated, he answered, "Wazz up?"

"Todd? Wha- are you at a party?" Hannah asked.

"Ye- kinda. I'ms on ze dock."

Hannah was silent. "You're drunk aren't you?"

"Yup." He was honest about it. On the end of the line he could hear Hannah crying. He asked, "What? What are you crying for?"

"I just...I just didn't expect this from you."

"Really?" Todd felt a sudden irritation. "Don't you blame me, though? Look at everything that's gone on. NOTHING is going the way it should. I've got nothing to live for here."

"That's not true. You-"

"Don't try to make me feel better. Truth be told, you left me here, despite how I felt. And honest, no- a long distance relationship won't work. So, instead of facing the inevitable on down the line, it's over. Goodbye, Hannah, have a wonderful life."

Todd hung up and turned off his phone. He almost even contemplated throwing it in the lake. What he said he knew was true, but couldn't admit it if it wasn't for the whiskey doing the talking for him. At least that's what his mind told him. And so, he took another swig, pulled himself up, and headed to the party.

The party was a whole new ball game to him; he wasn't sure what to do. And only having Hannah and Charlie by his side for so long, he didn't have anyone to turn to. Even so, nobody else had anything to do with him either. Todd was just another face in the crowd.

He shrugged it off, and headed to the exit when he ran into someone. They said, "Hey, watch it!"

Todd replied, "Sorry, Jill, I didn't see you."

"That whiskey has done some good for you hasn't it?" Ricky smiled from behind Jill and his arms wrapped around her waist.

"Psh, you know it." Todd chuckled.

"You leaving already?" Ricky asked.

"Yeah, this party is dead. See you guys later." Todd walked passed and took a quick glance at Stan who stood quietly behind his friends.

"Hold up, man," Ricky stopped him. "Why don't we all do something together? You want to ride with us?"

"Why not?" Todd shrugged.

They drove on through the night with a party of their own and passed liquor bottles back and forth between each other. Classic rock music blared from the radio with Todd and Stan in the back seat, Jill in the passenger seat, and Ricky driving. Todd really didn't say much, just observed everyone else- especially Stan who just sat and looked out the window with a gloomy look on his face.

"Mmm, so, Todd," Jill turned down the radio and lit a cigarette. "How's my *boyfriend* doing? He still locked up where he should be?"

"As far as I know, yeah. Charlie doesn't talk about him much." Todd said.

"Pfft. Well then. I hope he never gets out. If I ever saw him again, I swear I'll-"

Stan cut her off, "Hey, can we pull over here for a minute?" They pulled up to a gas station. "Wait for me, I'll only be a minute."

Ricky let the car idle as Stan went inside. Everything from then on was in slow motion. They could see Stan from inside the car walk up to the counter and pointed to cigarettes. But, with the cashier's back turned, Stan pulled out a revolver and aimed it at him.

"Oh crap, what's he-" Ricky leaned forward.

"Go get him, Rick, before he gets us all in deep-" Jill tried to say, but it was too late. The cashier had seen the revolver and grabbed a shotgun from underneath the counter and fired at Stan.

Jill yelled, "Get us out of here! Get us out of here! Drive! Drive! Drive!"

Ricky threw the car in reverse and spun out as he drove on. Todd saw the look on Stan's face as he was lifeless before he even hit the ground.

"What a moron! We're so dead!" Jill continued.

"Hang on, I'll get us out of here." Ricky was sure, but they didn't get far before they heard sirens in the distance.

The coffee shop where Charlie worked was coming up, and so Todd said, "Hey, just drop me off here."

Jill grabbed him by the collar before he climbed out and said, "You listen here, and you listen up good. Don't you dare even *think* about ratting us out. You are just as guilty as we are. And say you did, you won't live to see another day. Do you understand?"

Todd pushed her off, "Whatever, Jill, just don't ever lay your hands on me again." He left what was left of the whiskey in the backseat of the car.

Charlie watched everything from behind the counter as Todd shoved off Jill and stumbled in through the doors. He said, "Hey Todd, what are you-"

Todd went pale, threw up in the middle of the floor, and passed out.

***

Todd woke up the next morning in his own bed, with no recollection how he got there. The morning sun shined through his blinds and were much brighter than normal. And the pounding in his dead didn't help either. Which, to make matters worse, he felt vomit rising up his throat. He ran to the restroom and made it just in time.

Once his visit was all over with, he could hear Jim's voice echo from the doorway with a glass of Sprite and an aspirin, "Here, this should help."

"Thanks dad, I-"

Jim raised his hand and said, "Don't. Charlie told me everything that's been going on. Why didn't you come to me instead of riding around with those hoodlums? You could've been in jail right now, son. But, by God's grace, I got you from getting arrested. You-"

"Dad, please."

"No, Todd, you need to hear this. I'm not mad at you. I understand how you are feeling, but you are going about it all wrong. Son, that Stan boy, is dead. He's dead. That could've been you. And I know it's hard, but you need to give Hannah a call; she's worried sick about you. I know you both are heartbroken, but don't end it like this. Trust me."

Todd knew that his father was right, as much as he hated to admit it. He just couldn't leave it with Hannah that way. With what little money Jim had saved up for his college fund, he flew out to see her.

Chapter Twenty-Five

(2012)

Brad closed his bible, rubbed his hand against the well-worn leather binding, the same bible he had read every day since Charlie had given it to him. In prison, he had all the time in the world.

At first, he didn't know what to do with it. It didn't feel right in his hands, but he knew he had to have it for a reason. The moment he did contemplate reading it, he never put it down. And Logan had joined in as well. They each gave themselves to Christ and helped each other along the way. They'd read scripture back and forth to one another. In a funny way, it made prison enjoyable, peaceful.

Brad set the bible down on the bed just as Logan was accompanied to his cell by a guard and said, "You won't believe it- I'm set free. I'm going home!"

"Really? Logan, that's awesome, I'm happy for you."

"It's been a long time coming."

"Are you going back home?"

"You betcha." Logan smiled.

"Could you tell my brother something for me? Could you tell him…thank you?"

"I most certainly will do."

***

Charlie thought it was strange that instead of coming into work, Max wanted to meet him up at the court house. He followed Max inside and asked, "What's this about?"

"You'll see." Max said, now walking with a cane. "It's a surprise."

They didn't wait long. Max's attorney was in and out with the proper forms to sign. Before Charlie had known it, he was now the owner of the coffee shop; and with that, the name was changed to Dunzy's Coffee Shop. At 23 years old, Charlie's dream of owning a coffee shop had come true-God had surely blessed him well.

***

Coming back to town, everything looked different as Logan was now sober. He still couldn't help but think of his past, and all was quickly faded when he came upon Dunzy's Coffee Shop. Wow, how much the times have changed.

He made his way inside, expecting to see the same chubby Charlie as when he had last seen of him when he was just a kid himself. Except, the man behind the counter was built and had the same thick glasses as before. The glasses said it all. Logan sat down and said, "Man, you are a spitting image of your brother."

"That's a first. I've never heard that one before." Charlie looked at Logan puzzled; he couldn't place who he was.

"You don't remember me do you?"

"Sorry, but I don't."

"I'm your brother's friend, Logan." From the look on Charlie's face, Logan knew he was scared. "Whoa, hey, I come in peace. Honest."

"Sorry, it's just-no offense-any time you guys were around it always meant trouble. I don't need that right now."

"Well, I'm sorry about that. That was a long time ago. I'm done with all of that. And so is Brad."

"How do you know?"

"We spent time together the past five years. Brad's really come around, which he wanted me to tell you 'thank you'. Actually, we both want to thank you. Because of you, we found Christ."

"You're serious about this aren't you?" Charlie asked.

"Very. We all have had to grow up some time. I just got out, so I thought I'd drop in and say, hi. I saw the name and thought it had to be you."

"That's really great. Yeah, it was just signed to me the other day." Charlie knew he had to forgive them, in doing so, he asked, "Are you looking for a job? There's a spot open."

"Oh yeah, I've got to get on my feet somehow."

"Okay then, you're hired."

"Well then, that was easy." Logan laughed.

Chapter Twenty-Six

(2020)

Todd sat at his old desk in his bedroom, his legs barely fit underneath. On one side of his desk he had a cup of coffee, while on the other side sat an Ipod with the headphones attached to his ears. He typed away on his laptop and didn't hear the knock from the door.

He was lost in his own work and jumped from his seat when a hand grabbed his shoulder. "What the?!"

"Shh, it's just me." Aunt Lana said.

"You scared me half to death. What's wrong?"

"It's your father…"

He left everything where it was and rushed to his father's room. Jim's breathing was slow, and even still had a small smile on his face. He looked at Todd, weak, and said, "Hey, son."

"Hey dad." Todd sat down by him as Lana closed the door, leaving them alone. It took all Todd could do not to break down in tears. He knew that Jim was going, but it came on faster than he thought. Just the day before they were laughing and cutting up like it was nothing, and now…

"Working hard in…there?" Jim asked.

"Best I can be."

"Good…good."

Todd didn't know what to say, just held his father's fragile hand.

"Son…it's…okay…I'm..die-"

"Please, dad, don't say it. I know it's coming I just-"

"Don't…be…scared…I'm only…going… to Heaven…your mother…is…waiting…for…me."

"I know she is, it just hurts to let you go."

"Don't…be…selfish…punk." He managed yet another grin. "I'm happy…about…it."

"I will try, I'm happy spending time with you."

"No…here…" Jim slid his hand to Todd's heart. "Open

your...heart...to...God's...love...and...find...someone...to love...with...you...Love...is all...that...matters."

"I love you though, dad. You're all that I need."

Jim closed his eyes and said, "Hannah...she ma-...you...smile."

"I know she made me smile, but so do you."

"You're...stubborn."

"Eh, I get it from you." Somehow, through the pain, Todd smiled as well.

"I...love...you."

"I love you too, dad."

"...going...home...soon." His breathing went slower. "Good...b..."

Todd held his tears and stayed strong as much as he could. He kissed Jim's head and said, "Good bye, dad." He felt Jim's hand let go and go soft. Todd knew, he was gone.

Chapter Twenty-Seven

(2020)

"See ya, Charlie." Logan said, calling it a night.

"Alrighty, have a good night." Charlie locked the doors behind him and switched over the open sign. Dunzy's Coffee Shop was closed for the evening. He headed back to his office when his phone rang, he saw that it was Todd and answered, "Hey buddy, what's up?"

"Dad just passed away. Just thought I'd let you know."

"Oh man, I'm so sorry. I'm on my way."

Todd sat on the porch swing, smoking, when Charlie pulled up next to the hearse in the driveway.

"Hey, buddy." Charlie stepped up on to the porch and handed Todd a box of chocolates from Sassy Pants Sweets & Treats and took a seat next to Todd. "How are-"

Todd cut him off. "You don't have to ask how I am, 'cause I *don't* know how I am at the moment. But, thanks for coming I guess, you really didn't have to." He looked down at the box and continued, "You brought me chocolates? Really?"

"Hey, it's okay. You know your dad was like my dad also. And hey, don't dis the chocolate till you've tried it. They are my new sponsor and they are delicious - Sheri and Bobby know what's up."

"I know." Todd flicked his cigarette butt on to the yard. "I would offer you to come in and have a cup of coffee, but Lana and the funeral director are taking care of things."

"That's understandable. I guess they wouldn't want you to go berserk on them."

"Now would I do such a thing?"

"Hey, I've read your books...it's certainly possible."

"Good point." Todd looked at the ground for moment. He sighed and turned to Charlie to break the silence and said, "So, how's work?"

"Work's good. Busy, but good. How's your writing?"

"It's not bad. I haven't been writing as much as I should be, but being back home I've been able to breathe and catch up."

"See, I told you this place isn't so bad. We've had some good memories here."

"For you maybe...but for me, it ended bad."

"Hey, you've got some good memories as well Mr. Clinton. Do you remember our Lightsaber battle in the park? Or our late night video game nights?"

"Yeah, but, we were just kids then. We're all grown up now. Grown men."

"So? Who says we can't still be kids at heart?"

"Because...that's not how the world works."

"Well, you know what I say? Forget what the world says, or what the world does, and just do what makes you, *you*. The same *you* that God made you to be."

"You know the scary thing about that? That's basically what dad said to me before he passed, well, that I need to find someone that makes me happy."

"He's right though."

"How do you know? You aren't married. And as far as I know, you aren't seeing anyone either."

"Of course I'm married, I'm married to coffee. She's always there when I need her, and she makes me happy. She makes me warm when I'm cold. And even when I'm upset about something, her smell relaxes me."

"You're gonna have a heart attack one of these days, you know that?"

"Wellll that's what it takes to be married."

Todd didn't know why, but this made him laugh. He laughed so hard that Aunt Lana ran outside and asked, "What's wrong?"

"I think, Todd, may have gone crazy on us...well, more crazy than we already are." Charlie said with his eyes as wide as could be.

"I think I'm good now." Todd giggled. "Shew, I needed that."

"Umm, okay." Lana looked behind her as they were wheeling Jim through the hallway. "Todd, hunny, it's time."

He nodded, "Okay. I'll be fine right here. If anything was to happen, Charlie would sit on me."

"Gee, thanks." Charlie said.

"No problem, bud."

Lana couldn't say a word. She didn't know what came over Todd so quickly. Maybe that laugh was good for him. After all, laughter is the best medicine.

She held the door as they wheeled Jim out. Charlie kept his hand on Todd's shoulder for both support and a precaution.

"I'm good, Charlie, really."

Charlie stayed the rest of the night. They didn't sleep, but drank wine and reminisced on the old days. Todd stayed in a good mood, cheerful. It was like they were teenagers again. When Charlie left that morning, he scrolled through his phone until he came to the number he looked for and called.

"Well, good morning, Charlie, what are you calling this early for?" Hannah asked. "You didn't lock yourself out of the shop again did you?"

"No, not this time." Charlie hesitated. "It's Jim. He passed last night."

She was silent for a moment. "Thanks for telling me, I really appreciate it. Will you let me know when the funeral is?"

"Of course."

"Good. Does Todd know?"

"Yeah, he's here. I was with him all night. He's good, you know? Despite everything."

"That's good." She really didn't know what to say.

"He'll be really happy to see you, don't worry."

"Do you think so?" Hannah asked.

"I know so."

***

The funeral went well. A lot of town's people showed up- mostly church members, but that would've been okay with Jim. Todd handled everything well, he knew his dad was happy and knew that he was at rest. Even though, it hasn't dawned on him, yet, that Jim was gone, but that didn't come until after everyone had left. He said his goodbyes and then back to the parlor to look over his dad one last time.

As Todd stood over the body, he wanted so bad to wrap his arms around him and hug him, to feel his touch, but he knew that wish wouldn't come true. It was then that he really felt alone in the world, even more so when Aunt Lana would move back to her own house and that would just leave Charlie. Charlie wouldn't leave him for anything.

Then, out of nowhere, he thought of Hannah. It had been quite some time he even thought about her. Even though they didn't end on good terms, just the thought of her brought back all the old feelings he had for her. He knew then he had to find her, somehow.

His thoughts were interrupted with the clicking of heels on the hardwood floors behind him. Todd, turned to see Hannah standing in the doorway.

"Hi," Hannah said. She wasn't so sure what to say to him. Just seeing him caught her emotions off guard. For the first time in her life, she was nervous.

Todd looked down at his father and said, "You sneaky, sneaky old man. You're trying to tell me something, aren't you?"

With her arms crossed, she slowly walked toward him.

"Hey." He said to her, with a smile on his face.

She looked at Jim and put her hand on his, "He looks good, doesn't he?"

"Yeah…always has actually. Just frail in his old age." Todd sat down in the front row pew and loosened his tie. "I knew this day would come, but I was never emotionally prepared for it. Of course, I don't guess you could be when something like this just pops out of nowhere."

"No, I don't think you can, not fully anyways." Hannah sat beside Todd. "When God's ready to call you home, though, there's no stopping Him."

"Aint that the truth." Todd turned to Hannah and really looked at her. She was still as beautiful to him as the day they met. "Charlie called you didn't he?"

"He did. That's okay, isn't it? Don't be mad at him, he just thought it was best."

"No, that's perfectly fine with me. I'm not mad. You should be here."

Hannah nodded. "Good."

There was an awkward moment of silence between them. Todd then said, "Sorry I'm quiet, I'm not up for catching up at the moment. Sometime, though, just now right now. Thank you for coming."

"You're welcome." Hannah stood to walk out the door.

"Leaving already?"

"I took it you wanted to be alone."

"No," Todd said. "This may sound weird, but even after 12 years apart, out of all people, it's you who I'd rather just be with."

"Thank you, Todd." She sat back down and even though they didn't speak for a while, they held hands and just stared at Jim. And they would have stayed that way all night if the funeral director didn't make them leave, forcing them to go their separate ways for the night.

Chapter Twenty-Eight

(2020)

His last years in prison, Brad spent keeping only to himself. He didn't want anything to do with anybody, and all he wanted to do was keep cool and stay on the right path to righteousness.

When he found God, he found his true self underneath the anger and hate that had built up over the years. And so, at the age of 43, he was set free. By God's grace, the cell was open and Brad was going home.

***

They had partied hard, much harder than they ever did before. Reason being- it was Jill and Ricky's wedding night. It was only a court house wedding, in and out and on their way. And to them, it was the most amazing decision they could possibly make. They had been together for so long that it felt it was the right thing to do. And now, they celebrated the marriage with any known drug possible.

Ricky planned to make the night even more special. He said, "Baby, I love you. I have a surprise for yous. You're gonna love this. Guessss what I saw ats the court house today?"

"What…good lookin?" Jill stumbled.

"I saw our dear old, good pal, friend, buddy, buddy Brad walk out. He's freeee." Ricky flung his arms out like a bird, tripped over his own feet and fell face first to the ground. "Hello, Mr. Shaggy Carpet. How are you?"

"Whaaat? Why didn't you tell me sooner?" Jill punched the lamp on the night stand in their bedroom where it shattered to the floor. "Lets go get him. I told you I was going to get my revenge."

"Okay, just give me a min-" Ricky passed out cold and snoring.

"Really? On our wedding night? Ugh, men."

Chapter Twenty-Nine

(2020)

Only days after the funeral, Todd had all the windows open in his father's house. Knoxville, Tennessee weather was cold one week and warm the next and no in between. It was still winter, but felt like spring. Give it till next week when it will be cold again. The air was cool, so he let the breeze air out the stuffiness in the house. Aunt Lana had moved on, even though, she begged to help stay and clean; Todd wouldn't have it. She had done so much for Jim and so Todd, felt she needed a break and time for herself.

Which, now that Todd was home for good, he needed time himself to figure out what he was going to do with his life. All he had left to his name was his car and now his father's house. He hated to think of it like that, but that was the reality of it.

As he dusted, the sun set through the windows and he didn't notice the car pull in to the driveway. Then, when the knock came from the front door, he heard that. He figured it was more food from neighbors giving their condolences. His fridge was full enough as it was. He opened the door to see Hannah dressed in a Marvel Comics hooded sweatshirt, sweat pants, and Converse shoes. The same nerdy girl he fell for when they were kids.

"Well, hey." Todd said. "What's up?"

"Nothing…umm, would you like to get out for a while? Maybe go to Dunzy's Coffee Shop and just talk?"

"Yeah, sure. Let me get a shower real fast and we could go."

***

Charlie and Logan sat behind the counter in a massive Rock, Paper, Scissors game, but quiet enough not to disturb the old gentleman who read his bible at the other end of the counter. The gentleman was the only customer of the night, and to him, it was a sight to see grown men playing a harmless child's game and having fun. But of course, the harmless game quickly turned into a harmful one when the loser would get smacked in the face. The gentleman just smiled and shook his head.

When Todd pulled up with Hannah in the passenger seat, Charlie was the first to notice. He knew they weren't technically *together*, but it was still a joyful sight to see them together after all these years. He said to Logan, "Hey, follow my lead on something."

"Uh-oh, I know you. What are you going to do?"

Charlie gave an evil, mischievous grin and said, "Trust me."

Todd opened the car door for Hannah and also held the door for her when they entered in Dunzy's Coffee Shop.

Charlie screamed out as he imitated a game show host, "Welcome, my dear friends, to the one and only, extravagant, Dunzy's Coffee Shop and goodies from Sassy Pants Sweets & Treats. My name is Charlie Dunn, and here is my associate, Logan. Logan, why don't you tell these lovely folks about the place?"

"Well lets see," Logan said, "We have coffee, coffee, and oh yes, coffee."

"What else? What else do we have?" Charlie asked.

"We have tea."

"Yes tea."

"We have water."

"Yes of course, and water."

"We have all sorts of chocolatey goods from Sassy Pants Sweets & Treats."

"We do?"

"Yes sir, we do." Logan said.

"Okay, okay, what else?"

"They also do cakes, cookies and more!"

"More you say?"

"Much more! What else?"

"Umm, oh! We have a fireplace and chairs- leather chairs, comfy chairs, oh my!"

"Very good! Yes, we do have a fireplace for those lovely romantic evenings for you lovely adorable couples. Now, what could I get for you folks?" Charlie asked.

"Charlie..." Todd said.

"Yesss?"

"What in the world are you on? Did you put something in your coffee? I don't even know if I want anything now or not because of you two."

"Then why come to a coffee shop?" Logan asked.

"Yeah, why?" Charlie asked.

"Pft, I don't know. Ask the lady who came with me. She's the one who asked."

"Hey, I just thought it'd be a trip, which it must be 'cause you guys are trippin." Hannah stated.

"Word." Charlie threw up a peace sign.

"You guys have way too much time on your hands." Todd said.

"At least we're awesome about it." Logan laughed.

"Right, two coffees please, and hold the crazy." Todd said.

"Heyyyy!...okay." Charlie said. He enjoyed himself way too much.

Todd and Hannah took a seat by the fireplace. He asked, "I can't remember, was this here before? Since we've been gone I almost forgot what this place looked like."

"No, it was put in a couple years ago because of the ice storms Knoxville was hit with. Charlie thought the fire would be good for the power outages."

"Oh, that's good."

"Yeah." So many thoughts were running through Hannah's mind. She didn't know where to begin, but simply said, "So…"

"So…" Todd chuckled. "You'd think after all these years apart we'd have something to talk about."

"I wish it wasn't that long apart."

"Hey we tried, remember? I came out to you when you left for college and did everything I could to make it happen. I guess it just wasn't in God's plan at the time."

"But twelve years though, and no contact? What happened to you? What happened to *us*?"

Todd sighed. He knew one day he'd have to explain his actions. "Look, I'm going to tell you something that I've never told anyone, not even dad or Charlie. Two things had gone through my mind when I left you in New York: one, that we weren't meant to be like we thought, and two, was that if I couldn't make it there like I feared, then I wouldn't make it anywhere. I was terrified."

"But you made it, though, Todd. Look at where you are, you became a successful writer and are doing well for yourself. Aren't you?"

"Not really. After I left you, it about killed me, because it hurt so much I got lost in a world of drugs and booze. I went from couch to couch of a different 'friend' every night. The drugs helped kill the pain, and I was too ashamed to go home to ask for help. Too ashamed to ask for help from anybody. I was so deep in to my addictions that I completely forgot my entire life, I forgot who I was and where I had come from. I forgot everything.

For some reason one night I just started writing down my thoughts, which soon turned to stories. I'd go from one odd job to the next to get by, but would constantly write to the point I slowly forgot about the addictions. Then I went on one final binge and blacked out. When I came to, I was in a coffee shop and no clue where I was at. But there was *something* about the coffee shop that kept nagging at me. Finally, after some time of just sitting there, memories started flooding back where I remembered *everything* I forgot. I just couldn't do it anymore.

After that, I checked into a rehab center and then spent allot of the years after that trying to find *me* again and staying clean. In that time I started publishing my work. But, as hard as I tried, I couldn't figure out what was missing, why I couldn't feel complete. So I came home to start over and start fresh."

"Wow." Hannah sipped her coffee.

"Yeah, I wouldn't say I had an *easy* life. It's been a hard one to get here."

"I so didn't expect all that, I just assumed you came home because your dad was sick."

"Nope, I didn't even know about that. When we'd talk on the phone he was always cheerful. The only time I suspected anything was when Aunt Lana mention moving in to help out around the house. But I let that go."

"We didn't know either: Charlie and I. If we did, we would've let you know, so don't think we were trying to hide it from you."

"No, I wouldn't have thought that at all. Did you and Charlie keep in touch over the years?"

"Yes, we never stopped being friends. There has always been that brother/sister connection between us. I wouldn't have had it any other way."

"Honestly, it wouldn't have surprised me one bit if you and him had become a couple after I was gone. I would have figured you would be married and have a family by now."

"No, I couldn't. I did date here and there, but there wasn't any love. The only love I ever had was with you."

"I'm really sorry I wasn't there for you. You probably wasted all those years waiting on me and not being happy yourself."

"I did wait, Todd, but it wasn't a waste of my time. I finished school, graduated college, came back home and opened up a comic book store. I am happy, and just to have the chance to speak with you again makes me even more happy."

"That's really great, Hannah. I want you to know that-"

Todd was interrupted from a cool breeze as someone walked in the door.

"Welcome to Dunz-" Charlie began, but stopped in mid-sentence. "Brad?"

"Hey there, Charlie. Guess what? I'm free!" The two brothers embraced in a hug. "It's good to see you little brother. How are you?"

"I'm wonderful, wonderful! This is such a surprise!" Charlie turned and yelled at the back, "Logan! Look who's here!"

Logan walked in, "Whaaaat? Well, hey jail bird, you made it. Took you long enough."

"All in God's timing." Brad smiled.

"Very true. Want to know something even wild about that? As much trouble we caused Charlie, yeahhh, he's my boss now." Logan said.

"That's, Mr. Boss, to you." Charlie said.

Brad wiped tears and said, "Wow, a lot has changed."

"Much more than you think, turn around and you'll see my friend Todd Clinton from elementary school, he's a published writer now." Charlie pointed to Todd.

"I admit, I really don't remember you having any friends, I'm sorry."

"No, worries, he was the only one, until Hannah came along." Charlie put his arm around Brad's shoulder. "Come on, let me show you around."

The entrance door slammed open. Jill stumbled in and pointed to Brad, "There he is! I TOLD you he'd be here didn't?!"

Ricky walked in behind her and said, "Hey, Brad. Long time no see. You doing well?"

"No!" Jill yelled, "No, we're here to finish this. I told you I'd get my revenge on you, Brad. You remember? I know you do. No time for buddy, buddying right now."

"Yeah, what she said." Ricky snorted powder up his nose.

"Seriously? After all these years, you are still on that? Forget it, I'm an old man now. I'm done with all that. My life is for the Lord, not the streets." Brad said.

"Pft, please, you? I don't believe that one bit. You ditched us, remember? Nobody ditches us unless they want to face the consequences. And that means you." She pulled out a pistol from her back pocket, pointed it at Brad and looked around the room, continued, "Everyone else, I'd advise you to get out as fast as you can. This doesn't concern you."

"Jill, hey Jill, look who it is, it's that Todd kid we used to chum with that one time. And, and Logan? Wow, this is going to be a wild reunion." Ricky sounded like a child.

"Wellll, you were finally right about one thing, my foolish husband. In that case, lock the doors. NOBODY is getting out of here."

"Let 'em go, Jill, this has nothing to do with them. Only you and me." Brad insisted.

"Oh, shut up, Mr. Hero. I don't care who tastes my bullets tonight, as long as *you* taste them the most."

"Lets put the gun down Jill and talk about this. You don't know what you're doing. Brad is a changed man, he and I both. I know, I was there when we asked God into our lives." Logan said.

"This has nothing to do with whether or not he's changed! I could care less about that. What does matter, is that he. Ditched. Me. He was all I had and he ditched me. I loved you, Brad, and now I'm married to this Bozo." Jill said.

Ricky stood by her side picking his nose.

"I'm really sorry about that, Jill." Brad said, "I was stupid then. I'm sorry for a lot of things. But, if you loved me so much, why did you sleep with Ricky behind my back, instead of coming to see me in prison? You think this is all on me, but don't forget, you betrayed me as well. Eye for an eye."

"Don't you dare blame all of this on me! If you didn't have such daddy issues and wanted to be soooo big and bad, then you wouldn't be in this situation."

"You're right, but how is that situation any different from this one? Now it's you who's trying to be big and bad. Trust me, don't do this. I regret that day, dearly. If I could go back I'd forgive my dad then and there and move on with my life. But I can't. Don't put yourself in the same position I was in. Trust me."

"Which I accept your forgiveness, son." Everyone turned to the old gentleman at the counter.

"Dad?" Both Charlie and Brad asked at the same time.

"Yeah, boys, it's me."

"No!" Ricky yelled. Before they all could turn to see why, a gunshot echoed throughout the coffee shop. Ricky fell to the ground in a puddle of blood.

"Oh my-Look what you made me do, Ricky! You're such a clutz!" Jill dropped the gun and ran out the door.

"Someone call 911! Hurry!" Hannah was the first to administer CPR. But it was no use. Ricky was gone.

Chapter Thirty

(2020)

Minutes later, Jill was arrested when someone noticed her running down the street covered in blood. She confessed to the killing of Ricky and confessed to having intentions of killing Brad. But, because Ricky had jumped in front of the bullet, her plans were cut short.

This wasn't the welcoming party Brad had expected; which, he really didn't expect one in the first place. Everything just happened unplanned. And he didn't know *how* to relax his nerves. Going from jail, to home, to seeing his dad, and seeing an old friend die right in front of him really made a number on his nerves. He was on the verge of a nervous breakdown.

"We all need to get away." Charlie mentioned. "All three of us, just take a vacation, relax, and chat away."

"I know of a place." Bill said.

***

Dunzy's Coffee Shop was closed for three days while it took time for everyone to calm down and clean up the mess. But when they did open back up, it was up to Logan and Todd to run the place.

"Hey, can you believe it?" Todd asked Hannah as she walked in. "I'm helping run a coffee shop. Who would've thought? Dad surely would've been proud."

"He would've had to taste your coffee first." Logan poured out a full mug of coffee.

"Heyyyy." Todd said.

"Are you guys busy?" Hannah asked. Something was bothering her.

"Na, we just made it through the morning rush. We should be good for another couple of hours or so." Logan said.

"Okay. Could I speak with you a minute, Todd?"

"Yeah, sure." They walked outside to the patio tables and had a seat. "What's up?"

"I just wanted to finish our conversation from the other night. I want to know something; did you forget about me when you left? I mean, have you thought about me any?"

"I did think about you any chance I got. I forgot a lot of the memories for a while when I wasn't in my right mind, but I still thought about you. Why do you ask?"

"Because ever since I saw you at your dad's funeral I can't stop thinking about you. When I saw you, it was a flood of emotions of how much I always loved you. And I just can't help but think that since we last saw each other that you fell out of love with me."

"No, Hannah, I *never* stopped loving you. Good or bad, you were always on my mind."

"Then, why, for all these years did you not call or write me once? Or even one text or email? If you loved me so much, why leave me in the wind?"

"Because I was ashamed, Hannah. Look at where I was. It broke my heart because I didn't know if things would ever be the same. In the beginning, no I didn't want to get better. The drugs had me strong, but then afterwards, I figured you moved on."

"Okay." She looked away with tears in her eyes. "What about now? Where are we now?"

***

They stopped by Max's Diner for lunch. Charlie and Bill took their time savoring the food, but Brad, on the other hand, scarfed it all down in only minutes. And he ordered more. It had been so long since he had real greasy American food that he had forgotten how addictive, mouth-watering it could be. He knew it wouldn't end well, but he kept on devouring plate after plate.

Sure enough, it didn't take long for the food to digest. As Bill and Charlie stood outside, taking in the Christy, Tn scenery, they waited for Brad to leave the restroom.

***

"We're at Dunzy's Coffee Shop." Todd smiled, being funny.

"Todd…"

"I'm sorry, had to be done." Todd took a breath. "One of the last things my dad told me before he died was to be happy. And I never really was truly happy unless I was with you. Which explains why I'm so happy now, even though it hasn't even been two weeks since dad, but because I'm with you. Where I see us now-well hoping-is to start over. It'd be just you and I the way it should've been-the way it should've been all along, but I'm guessing the time apart was God's test in our patience and faith for Him. Though, yes, I failed that miserably, He still never gave up on us and here we are today."

"You're right though, we really don't know what His reasons are, but everything always works out best for Him. Which, if I'm taking it correctly, if you are wanting to start over, then we definitely should. After everything that has gone on in the past few weeks, I have come to realize just how short life really is. And I don't want to waste any second living it without you in my life."

"Which, hey, I couldn't complain about that. I say lets go for it and make it official."

"Yeah?"

"Yes ma'am." He leaned in and kissed her with a kiss so passionate they didn't let go for quite a bit.

"Wow...I've missed that. I certainly can't deny the sparks between us."

"Pst, more like fireworks."

"Yes!"

***

"Dad, where are you taking us? I feel like you are taking us through the town in *Children of the Corn*. That's what it sure looks like." Brad said.

"Far from it. This here is Christy, Tennessee. It's quiet, peaceful, and friendly. A home away from home."

"More like a home away from a slasher film." Charlie said.

"How could we not know about this place? We're practically next door to them from Knoxville." Brad asked.

"They like to stay secluded, off the grid as much as possible. Keeps down the tourism." Bill said.

"Yeah, that's not creepy at all." Charlie whispered.

Bill turned to Charlie and smiled, he knew where his sense of humor came from.

They pulled into a gravel parking lot beside a small white church that was surrounded by a white picket fence and a graveyard. A gentleman in a Hawaiian shirt and tan shorts stepped out from the front door and waved, "Good afternoon, Bill!"

"Afternoon, Reverend Brown. How are you?"

"Mighty fine today. Beautiful weather isn't it?"

"Yes, sir it is, yes sir. There's a couple of fellas I'd like you to meet- my boys."

Reverend Brown smiled the biggest of smiles. "Lovely, heavenly father, our God is great! Boys, your daddy has been praying for the day to see you all again for many years. Ask and you shall receive. Thank the Lord. Come in, come in, lets all have a chat." He stepped out of the way to let them in and said, "So, what brings y'all around, Bill?"

"Well, Brad just came home from prison, and was attacked the other night at Charlie's shop. We all just wanted to take a retreat for a little while and get to know each other again. For once in our life, be a family."

"And a fine place to start, I shall say."

"Very true reverend. I'd like for you to help us in the same way you had helped me before."

He placed his hands on Bill's shoulder. "It'd be an honor."

Epilogue

(One Year Later)

Newlyweds, Todd and Hannah Clinton drove to Christy, Tennessee with their windows down letting in the summer air. They held their hands with their fingers perfectly intertwined with one another. A Star Wars soundtrack played on the radio.

They didn't know what to expect when they arrived to town, just followed Charlie's instructions to the big surprise.

Charlie made sure everything was perfect before he opened the new shop. Townsfolk were already gathered outside on the sidewalk upon the arrival of Christy County's first coffee shop- Dunzy's Coffee Shop.

Todd and Hannah parked and walked up the sidewalk themselves. When he saw the crowd, he knew he was at the right place.

It was time, Charlie unlocked the door and flipped over the open/closed sign and welcomed in his customers. One by one they slowly entered and took in the aroma of fresh brewed coffee and the crackling of fire in the fireplace and gazed at the many Sassy Pants Sweets & Treats chocolates, cakes, and cookies in the display case. Everyone was certainly in awe.

"Welcome to Dunzy's Coffee Shop. Free samples await you. Enjoy." Charlie smiled at how happy his fellow town's people were. This was home. His smile grew even bigger when he saw Todd and Hannah walk in and continued, "Hey guys! Thank you for coming by. Surprise! How do you like it?"

"Charlie, this...is so elegant and fantastic. So much bigger than your other place." Hannah's eyes wandered.

"Thank you. I really love it. I see you guys made it okay."

"Oh yeah, it was easy to get here. Practically just one way." Todd said.

"See, I told you, well, stick around, let me help my customers and I'll be right back with you."

"Take your time, no worries."

Todd and Hannah cuddled up on the couch by the fireplace and watched how happy and glowing Charlie was behind the counter. He was surely blessed, and they were happy for him. when the last customer was out the door, Charlie practically skipped with joy to his friends and said, "Wow, that was awesome! Sure, I get that every day, but still, I love it."

"We can tell man, we're so proud of you." Todd gave him a high five.

"You really are so happy. It's noticeable." Hannah said.

"Thanks guys." Charlie sat down. "So, how are you liking the married life? Haven't killed each other yet, I see."

"Oh no, it's amazing. Especially the wedding cake that Sheri & Bobby made for us. It was a dream come true – this all is. I think we are all where we are meant to be-where God wanted us to be. And it's really showing through our smiles." Hannah said.

"I truly believe that, because Todd remembers how dark my childhood was at first. And then, after he and I met, steps were taken to a better life. Which, you all surely know how many years it took to be happy. But God always knows what He's doing."

"Amen to that." Todd smiled.

"You know what's weird? We're 32 years old and yet I feel like we're 12 again. I feel just like it was when it was just us in the back of the classroom. There was a certain peace with us then."

"That's not weird at all. It makes sense really, going along with what we were saying about how we're where we are meant to be. I believe that, because we are living by and for God. It just goes to show that no matter what goes on in life, we *have* to live by His ways and He will guide our paths. It all comes down to how we live in His name."

"And that, ladies and gentlemen, is why I love my wife." Todd laughed.

"I agree with you. This is the first time since the retreat with my dad and Brad that I feel complete. Granted, not long after that dad died, but I'm glad we all came together with love and forgiveness. Now, as you know, I am here, and Brad is home running the other shop, and you guys are married. My life is surely blessed, which I'll say that my life really didn't start until I met you guys. Thank you for being there for me." Charlie said.

"We'll always be here, man. Every day is a new chapter in our lives. We will always be friends."

"Speaking of a new chapter, just like you took me under your wing, Todd, I met this kid awhile ago named Michael Gable. Right now, he works at the other shop, but he'll soon be moving here. I saw a lot of me in him, and so the tables have turned and I'll protect him, like you protected me." Charlie said.

Hannah raised her mug to the air, "It's a blessing one cup of coffee at a time."

"It doesn't end there." Charlie walked behind the counter, bent down out of sight, and came back up with two toy Lightsabers.

Todd gave a look at Hannah that said, *'Can I?'*. She smiled and said, "Go head and play."   While the men played, she sat back by the fire and watched the two men she loved, smiled, and said to herself, "Yep, God is great."

ABOUT THE AUTHOR

R.E. Henderson is a Christian author from Knoxville, Tennessee along with his wife and painter, Rachel Henderson. They live with their daughter and 4 crazy dogs.

www.r-e-henderson.com

Sponsors

Sassy Pants Sweets & Treats

Pedal Java

http://pedaljava.com/

Other books by R. E. Henderson:

Expect the Unexpected

Seek

Lessons of an Old Fashioned Life

Confused: Greatest Hits